FHM

# Also By Jim Eldridge

# JIM ELDRIDGE

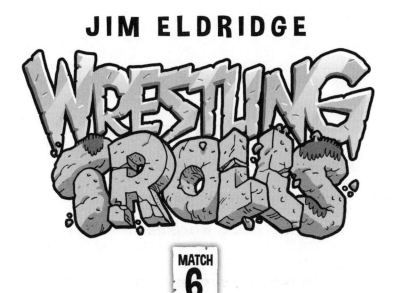

## MATCH 6

# THE FINAL SHOWDOWN

Illustrated by JAN BIELECKI

HOT
KEY
BOOKS

First published in Great Britain in 2015 by Hot Key Books
Northburgh House, 10 Northburgh Street, London EC1V 0AT

A CIP catalogue record for this book is available from the British Library.

ISBN: 978-1-4714-0269-2

1

This book is typeset in 14pt Sabon using Atomik ePublisher

Printed and bound by Clays Ltd, St Ives Plc

www.hotkeybooks.com

Hot Key Books is part of the Bonnier Publishing Group
www.bonnierpublishing.com

# Contents

# MOUNT DOOM

# CHAPTER 1

'My lords, ladies and gentlemen!'

The voice of the referee boomed around the arena, quieting the crowd, bringing an expectant hush. The two wrestlers were already in their corners of the ring: in the red corner stood the tiny figure of the Masked Avenger, dressed in her red costume with her full-face red mask hiding the fact that she was really Princess Ava, the teenage ruler of Weevil. Her mask could only be removed and her true identity revealed if she were beaten in a bout. So far, no one had beaten her. But now she was up against her toughest opponent yet.

'Tonight's top-of-the-bill bout is for the Lightweight Wrestling Championship,' continued the referee. 'In the blue corner, the defending champion, Crusher Clarice.'

At this, a huge section of the crowd erupted into loud cheering, foot-stamping and whistling, with slogans and banners waving.

Clarice bounced into the centre of the ring, waving at her supporters to acknowledge their cheers. She was much taller than the Masked Avenger, her arm and shoulder muscles bulging beneath her shiny silver-and-gold costume.

'Clarice is *really* good,' whispered Jack nervously.

Jack was in the front row with Milo and Meenu, just below the Masked Avenger's corner. Robin the old horse and Blaze the phoenix had been barred from the arena because of a notice that said: NO ANIMALS ALLOWED INSIDE.

'That's discrimination!' Robin had exploded angrily at the attendant. 'Say I was a wrestling horse taking part in a bout!'

'Are you?' the attendant had asked.

'Well . . . no,' admitted Robin.

And so Robin had been forced to stay outside. Blaze had sneakily transformed himself into a tiny mouse and smuggled his way inside hidden in Jack's top pocket, from where he was able to watch the match.

Out of the corner of his eye, Jack saw Big Rock and Hunk work their way through the crowd to join them.

Hunk was a half-troll, but he was only troll from the knees down, with the biggest, toughest feet ever. From his knees upwards, he was not just human, he was a very handsome human. He was so good-looking that Jack and Milo and the Masked Avenger hadn't liked him when they'd first met him, thinking he must be very vain. But they discovered that he was actually a really nice person, kind and caring, proud to be a half-troll, and determined to be a great wrestler. They hadn't seen Hunk for a while, but today they'd met up at this wrestling tournament, and when Hunk told them his partner for a tag-match had fallen ill, Big Rock had quickly volunteered.

'Me and Hunk make good team,' he'd said.

And they did. Big Rock and Hunk had won their bout, a Trolls versus Orcs tag-team contest, and were returning after changing out of their wrestling costumes.

'Crusher and Masked Avenger,' grunted Big Rock, sitting down next to Jack. 'Good wrestling!'

As the cheering for Crusher Clarice died down, the referee again took to the centre of the ring.

'And introducing the challenger in the red corner, ladies and gentlemen . . . the Masked Avenger!'

As the Masked Avenger strode to the centre of the ring, Jack and the others stood up, cheering and shouting, but their voices were lost in the roar from a large section of the rest of the audience.

'The Masked Avenger's popular with more than just us,' smiled Meenu.

As the Masked Avenger returned to her corner, the referee reminded everyone of the rules: two pinfalls, two submissions or a knockout would decide the winner. Then the bell sounded, and the Masked Avenger and Crusher Clarice moved out of their corners.

It was obvious from the wariness of both wrestlers as they circled one another that each had great respect for the other.

'Clarice is bigger, but the Masked Avenger's faster,' whispered Jack.

'No,' disagreed Milo. 'I've seen Clarice wrestle before, and she is very fast as well.'

To back up his point, as the Masked Avenger dived at Clarice, the Crusher swayed aside at the last moment, darting nimbly back to a safe distance.

The Avenger skidded to a stop, turned, and dived towards Clarice. Clarice let the Masked Avenger crash into her, and then suddenly somersaulted forwards, at the same time grabbing the Avenger round the waist.

The speed of the move, combined with the Crusher's weight advantage, caught the Masked Avenger off-balance, and she found her shoulders pinned to the canvas, held down by the weight of the Crusher lying on top of her.

'One! Two! Three!' called the referee, and the crowd went wild, shouting and cheering as Clarice bounced off the Avenger and danced back to her corner.

'That was one of the fastest pinfalls I've ever seen,' muttered Meenu, worried.

'That's why Crusher's the Champion,' said Milo. 'She's big and fast and strong.' He shook

his head. 'I think the Avenger could finally be unmasked in this match.'

Crusher Clarice came out of her corner fast, obviously intending to bring the match to a swift end. The Avenger dodged to one side, letting the Crusher hurtle past her, but one of Clarice's long arms grabbed hold of the Masked Avenger's shoulders as she did so, spinning the Avenger around. As the Masked Avenger stumbled and then recovered her balance, the

Crusher repeated the move that had won her the first pinfall: somersaulting forwards, and at the same time grabbing the Avenger round the waist.

But this time the Avenger was prepared, and as Clarice flipped the Avenger upside down, the Masked Avenger used the speed of the Crusher's attack to continue with a momentum of her own, rolling forwards and doing her own somersault, which brought Clarice sailing over the Avenger's head and crashing shoulder-first into the canvas.

*CRUNCH!*

The Avenger wrapped herself around Clarice like a human net and used her own weight to keep Clarice's shoulders pinned to the canvas.

'One! Two! Three!'

The arena erupted into wild shouts and cheers as the two disentangled and the referee ordered them to their corners.

'Two pinfalls in just a few seconds!' exclaimed Milo, awed. 'This is the fastest match I've ever seen!'

'Avenger good,' nodded Big Rock. 'She win!'

'I'm not sure,' said Hunk, concerned. 'Clarice is the stronger. The longer this goes on, the more chance Clarice has of winning.'

After those first two fast pinfalls, the match began to stretch out as first the Crusher and then the Masked Avenger seemed to take the upper hand.

'This is edge-of-the-seat stuff,' said Jack nervously, sitting on the edge of his seat.

It began to look as if Hunk might be right. Crusher Clarice's extra strength seemed to be slowly wearing the Masked Avenger down. The Crusher threw the Masked Avenger out of the ring on two occasions – both times the Avenger only just made it back to the ring in time to beat the referee's count.

Then the Crusher threw the Masked Avenger over her shoulder with such force that when the Avenger hit the canvas, the whole arena echoed with the sound. The Avenger lay there, dazed, her eyes closed. Clarice smiled and threw herself on the Avenger, but at the last second the Masked Avenger rolled away, and as Clarice hit the canvas, the Avenger grabbed her, rolled her onto her back and then performed a handstand that ended with the Masked Avenger dropping both knees onto Clarice's shoulders, pinning them down.

Frantically, Clarice bucked, trying to throw the Avenger off, her boots and knees sending kicks aimed at the Avenger – but the Masked Avenger kept her head down and her knees firm.

'One! Two! Three!' counted the referee.

As he finished his count, the whole audience leapt to their feet, shouting and stamping and whistling and roaring in appreciation of the two wrestlers. The referee struggled to make himself heard – he had to shout as he made the announcement: 'The new Lightweight Wrestling Champion is . . . the Masked Avenger!'

The crowd continued to go ballistic, shouting and roaring and cheering.

In the ring, Crusher Clarice gave the Avenger a hug of congratulation, then held the Avenger's arm aloft to declare her victorious.

'That's a really nice sporting gesture,' said Meenu.

'Crusher good person,' said Big Rock.

'Indeed she is,' nodded Hunk. 'She's always been supportive of up-and-coming wrestlers.'

Milo ran forward to greet the Avenger with a hug as she climbed down from the ring.

'Congratulations!' said Jack, hugging her as well.

'I couldn't have done it without the support of you guys,' said the Avenger.

As the others clustered around her, Hunk said, 'I think we should go outside to let Robin know that the Masked Avenger won. He's the only one who couldn't come in.'

'Absolutely!' said Milo.

They headed up the aisle towards the exit, the Masked Avenger having to stop every few steps as she was congratulated by delighted fans. Finally they made it outside, where they found Robin waiting impatiently for them.

'At last!' snorted the old horse.

'The Masked Avenger won!' said Milo.

'Yes, I heard the result already,' said Robin. 'But you need to know about this!' And he gestured towards a messenger pigeon that was nearby, pecking at some seeds it had found in the grass. 'It's got a message for Jack.'

Jack frowned, curious, and hurried over to the messenger pigeon. A piece of paper with the word 'Jack' on it had been strapped to its leg.

'I'm Jack,' Jack said to the pigeon.

The pigeon held out its leg and Jack unstrapped the piece of paper and opened it out.

'What's it say?' asked Milo.

Jack read it, then looked at them, shocked. He read the message aloud: 'Help. I am a prisoner in Castle Dark on Mount Doom. Save me. Your grandfather, Lord Veto.'

# CHAPTER 2

'Who could have taken Lord Veto prisoner?' asked Hunk.

'It must be the Voyadis,' said Princess Ava. 'They were the ones who were after him before, because he owed them money.'

The Voyadis were a very rich, very secretive and very, *very* dangerous crime family.

'That doesn't make sense,' said Jack. 'They got their money back when they took Veto Castle from him. Why lock him up now?'

'As an example to anyone else thinking of not paying the Voyadis,' said Ava. 'This is what happens to people who try to cross them.'

'Maybe,' said Meenu thoughtfully. 'But doesn't it strike you as odd that Lord Veto is supposed to be a prisoner in this Castle Dark, and yet he's managed to get hold of a pigeon to send Jack a message?'

'Good point,' said Ava. 'But why would anyone pretend to be a prisoner?'

'Because he's setting a trap,' said Milo.

'Why?' asked Jack.

'Who knows?' said Milo. 'Because he's Lord Veto, and very sneaky and not to be trusted. Maybe he wants to get hold of you and make you turn into Thud for some reason. Some *crooked* reason. Face it, Jack, Lord Veto may be your grandfather, but he's never done anything good for you, ever. The exact opposite. He kept you as a slave in his kitchens. He starved you and made your life a misery. And then he threw you out!'

'On a cold, rainy morning,' added Robin.

'Yes, all that's true,' admitted Jack. 'But he is my grandfather, and if he *is* in trouble I have to do my best to rescue him.'

'Why?' demanded Milo. 'Didn't you hear what we said? He was horrible to you! This

Castle Dark sounds the best place for him. He deserves to be locked up!'

'Because, for all that, he's the only family I've got.'

'Only because he killed your father and mother!' burst out Milo.

'Not on purpose . . .' said Jack, though he didn't sound very convinced by his own argument.

'Lord Veto caused their deaths!' insisted Milo. Then he added: 'Anyway, I thought *we* were your family. Me, Big Rock and Robin.'

'Yes, you are,' said Jack. He sighed. 'I'm sorry. I think I'm confused.' He looked at the message again. 'I didn't expect to get anything like this.'

'Let's talk to the pigeon,' suggested Ava. 'It may be able to tell us more about this.'

'Good idea,' nodded Jack.

He went to where the pigeon was feeding on some seeds.

'Excuse me . . .' he began.

The pigeon looked up at him.

'Coo?' it asked.

Jack frowned.

'Can you talk?' he asked.

'Coo coo,' said the pigeon.

'What language is that?' asked Milo.

'It's Bird language,' said Blaze. 'Leave this to me.'

The phoenix began to talk to the pigeon in a series of clicks and sounds that were a mystery to Jack and the others. The pigeon nodded, and replied in the same language, adding to it with a mime, flapping its wings and pointing with a foot.

'The pigeon says Lord Veto was really, really upset,' translated Blaze. 'He says it's a two-day journey to Mount Doom. It's a high peak in the Dead Mountains in the Kingdom of Fog.'

'The Dead Mountains in the Kingdom of Fog!' sniffed Robin. 'This place sounds worse and worse!'

'Ask him if he actually got this message from Lord Veto and if he's on his own,' urged Jack.

Once more, Blaze made a series of clicks and strange sounds at the pigeon, who nodded and replied in the same language.

'That nod looked like a yes to me,' said Milo.

'It was,' confirmed Blaze. 'Lord Veto is locked up in a room at the top of a high tower in this Castle Dark and he gave this pigeon the message himself. His orc, Warg, is with him.'

'Good old faithful Warg,' said Hunk. 'Everyone should have a friend.'

'Does the pigeon know who the people are who are keeping Lord Veto prisoner?' asked Milo.

'No,' replied Blaze. 'He says he was minding his own business, pecking at some seeds, when a sack was thrown over him. The next second, he was being carried through the air. After a long while, he was thrown into a room, and when the sack was opened he saw Lord Veto and Warg in there. He recognised Lord Veto because he'd carried messages for him before.'

'So he didn't see anyone else except for Lord Veto and Warg?'

Blaze talked to the pigeon again, and the pigeon replied.

'He saw some ninjas in the castle courtyard as he flew away with the message to find Jack.'

'Ninjas – the Voyadis' personal warriors!' exclaimed Ava. 'That clinches it! I was right! It *is* the Voyadis who are behind this!'

'Right,' said Jack determinedly. 'My mind is made up! I'm going to Castle Dark to rescue my grandfather!'

'Me come too!' shouted Big Rock.

'And me!' added Hunk.

'Absolutely,' agreed Blaze.

They turned to look questioningly at the others.

'Oh, well,' sighed Milo. 'We are a family, and families should stick together.'

'Count us in, too,' said Ava. 'Me and Meenu.'

They all now turned to look at Robin.

'Huh!' snorted the old horse. 'I never thought the day would come when I'd put myself at risk for Lord Veto!'

'You don't have to come,' said Jack. 'I won't be angry.'

'I should hope not!' said Robin. 'But if you think you're going off and leaving me all alone, you can think again!'

# CHAPTER 3

Early next morning the convoy set off for Mount Doom: Jack and Milo on the driving seat of their wagon, with Meenu and Princess Ava's caravan following just behind. Big Rock and Hunk ran alongside the caravans, with Blaze flying overhead. Now they knew the Voyadis were involved, they kept alert for any sign of trouble. But, by the time they made camp that night, their journey had been without incident.

'So far, so good,' said Milo as he and Jack lit a fire to cook their evening meal over.

'I still don't like it,' said Robin, watching and listening. 'It's too easy. If the Voyadis have taken Lord Veto prisoner, why haven't they tried to stop us coming to his rescue?'

'It must be a trap,' said Meenu. 'I don't think they want to stop us. They want us to get to this Castle Dark. They're using Lord Veto as bait.'

'Perhaps the Voyadis don't actually know we're on our way,' said Hunk.

'The Voyadis know everything,' said Ava. 'That's why they're so rich and powerful.' She looked at Jack. 'I bet they know all about that Royal Troll Ring of yours. And that you're the heir to the Troll Kingdom. I bet that's what this is all about! They want to use you in some way.'

'I reckon we should let the Voyadis have Lord Veto,' snorted Robin.

'Like I said before, I understand how you feel, Robin, and I won't hold it against you if you decide not to carry on,' said Jack.

'Who said I wasn't going to carry on!' exploded Robin indignantly.

'You said –' began Hunk.

'I was just giving an opinion! I never said I wouldn't carry on. For one thing, if I left, who'd pull the caravan?'

'Me,' offered Big Rock.

'Huh!' snorted Robin. 'This caravan is old. It needs to be pulled along gently and carefully. You'd wreck it.'

Jack and Meenu prepared a meal of hot stew and, as daylight faded and turned to night, they all sat down to eat.

'I was thinking, Jack,' said Milo, between mouthfuls of stew, 'if Ava's right and this is about that Troll ring of yours: why? What's so special about it?"

'It royal ring,' said Big Rock.

'Yes, but there might be more to it than that.'

'You ought to wear it, Jack,' said Hunk. 'It shows who you are. The Troll Prince.'

Jack hesitated.

'I don't know,' he admitted at last. 'It's very special. It belonged to my father, and my mother left it for me.'

'All the more reason to wear it,' said Milo. 'If I had a royal ring, I'd wear it to show it off.'

'Jack isn't you,' said Ava. 'Jack doesn't show off.'

'But it's something to be proud of,' insisted Milo. 'It seems a shame to keep it hidden.'

Jack thought it over.

'Yes, I suppose you're right,' he said. 'It's just . . . it's very precious to me. I don't want anything to happen to it.'

'If you keep it on your finger, you know it'll be safe, because you'll always be able to see it.'

Again, Jack thought it over.

'Yes, that makes sense,' he admitted.

'Everyone then see Jack true king,' nodded Big Rock.

'But that's the thing!' burst out Jack. 'I don't want everyone knowing that! If people know you're a king or a prince, they act differently towards you, instead of treating you like an ordinary person.'

'But you're not an ordinary person, Jack,' pointed out Hunk gently. 'You're a half-troll, and you're the heir to the Troll throne. That makes you special.'

'That may be so, but I sympathise with Jack,' said Ava. 'Look at me. If everyone knew when

I wrestled that I was really Princess Ava of Weevil, they'd act differently towards me.'

'More people would come to see you wrestle,' said Milo hopefully. 'We could make a lot of money.'

'You're wrong, Milo,' said Meenu. 'People come to watch the Masked Avenger because they hope to see her lose and have her mask taken off so they can find out who she is. It's the mystery about her identity that brings the crowds in.'

'Plus the fact that she's one of the best wrestlers ever,' said Hunk.

'Thank you, Hunk!' smiled Ava.

'Getting back to the ring,' said Milo impatiently. 'Can't we see you with it on just

this once? After all, we're your friends. We know you and we won't treat you differently.'

'Yes,' said Robin. 'I'd like to see that: Jack wearing the royal ring.'

'True Troll King,' nodded Big Rock. 'Be good to see.'

They all looked appealingly at Jack.

'Just this once?' asked Milo again.

'All right,' said Jack. 'Just for you. And to see how it feels.'

He took the ring from his pocket, examined it lovingly, and then slid it on his finger.

The effect was instantaneous and stunning. Where before there had been small, frail Jack, now the giant figure of Thud the Troll stood, towering over all of them as they stared up at him, open-mouthed.

'Wow!' croaked Robin.

Thud pulled off the ring and immediately transformed back into thin little Jack.

'I turned into Thud!' he gasped.

'Yes, you did,' nodded Ava, still stunned.

'King Thud!' said Big Rock, awed.

'That was fantastic!' exclaimed Milo. 'Can I have a go?'

'Er –' began Jack doubtfully, but Milo had already snatched up the ring and put it on his finger.

They all watched Milo, waiting for the change to come over him. But nothing happened.

Milo took the ring off, disappointed, and handed it back to Jack.

'It doesn't work on me,' he sighed.

'That's because you're not even a little bit of a troll,' said Ava. 'Jack's a half-troll, remember.'

'Well, if it works on half-trolls, let Hunk try it on,' suggested Milo.

Hunk shook his head.

'No,' he said. 'It's the Royal Troll Ring. Only a royal troll should wear it.'

'But we just want to see if it works on other half-trolls and turns them into whole trolls, like it does with Jack,' said Meenu.

Hunk shook his head again.

'I don't know,' he said. 'Say it does? That means it's dangerous, because every half-troll will be after it.'

'Which is why we have to find out,' said Ava.

Hunk looked uncertainly at Jack.

'It doesn't seem right, Your Majesty,' he said.

'I'm not Your Majesty,' protested Jack. 'I'm just Jack!' He held out the ring to Hunk. 'But it would be good to know if it does work on other half-trolls.'

Hunk hesitated.

'If it does, I'm worried about what sort of troll I might turn into,' said Hunk. 'I mean, I like being a half-troll just as I am. But if I became a whole troll, I could be a very angry one, like Thud.'

'Or you could be a nice one, like Big Rock,' pointed out Meenu.

Again, Hunk hesitated. Then he nodded.

'All right,' he said. He took the ring from Jack and slipped it on one of his fingers.

The others watched him eagerly, looking out for any signs of change. But, as with Milo, there were no changes at all. Hunk stayed looking exactly the same.

He took the ring off and handed it back to Jack.

'Maybe it's lost its power,' suggested Ava.

'Only one way to find out,' said Jack, and he put the ring back on his finger.

Immediately, tiny Jack was replaced by the towering figure of Thud, the giant Troll. Thud let out a huge roar, then took the ring off and became Jack again.

'Well, there's the answer,' said Meenu. 'It only works for Jack.'

'That because Jack true Troll King,' said Big Rock.

'That's what it must be,' said Ava. 'The ring recognises something in your blood, or your body, that you got from your father, the Troll Prince, and that triggers the change.'

'Well, at least we now know you can control when you turn into Thud,' said Milo. He smiled.

'Which means rescuing Lord Veto is going to be a lot easier!'

Princess Ava shook her head.

'Not necessarily,' she said, a worried look on her face.

'Why?' asked Hunk.

'Because, as Meenu said, this is obviously a trap the Voyadis have set to get Jack to this Castle Dark. They must know about the ring, and that it's got some sort of magic power, and they want to get their hands on it.'

'But we've just seen that it only works on Jack!' said Milo.

'We can't be sure of that,' said Ava. 'Say there's another relative of the Troll Royal Family out there, another half-troll, like Jack?'

'Unlikely,' frowned Blaze. 'Jack's unique.'

'Unlikely, but not impossible,' insisted Ava.

'Well, I guess there's only one way to find out,' said Jack. 'We go into the trap and see what happens.'

# CHAPTER 4

They met no one on their journey the next morning. The road climbed upwards, and Robin had to pull harder to haul the caravan, with Big Rock and Hunk adding their strength to push both caravans uphill. Finally, just after midday, the convoy arrived at the foothills of a mountain range shrouded in thick mist.

'Let me guess,' said Robin. 'This must be the Kingdom of Fog. And those must be the Dead Mountains.'

'What a desolate place,' said Meenu. 'Do you think anyone actually lives around here?'

'We're on a road, which must go somewhere,' said Milo. 'And we know there's a castle ahead.'

They continued on, and as the road climbed

higher, twisting and turning through the mountains, the mist and fog began to diminish and they heard the sound of rushing water.

'There must be a river,' said Jack.

They negotiated another uphill bend in the road, and then stopped. After the gloomy landscape they'd journeyed through, they had come upon a beautiful green patch of land, with about fifty houses nestling in it. Smoke rose from the chimneys.

'This is a surprise,' said Ava.

They saw that the road ahead of them forked: the left-hand fork leading to the small village; the right fork towards the river. And on the other side of the river a mountain rose up, with a castle at the very top.

'Any bets that's Mount Doom and Castle Dark?' asked Ava.

They followed the fork in the road towards the river and then stopped. The bridge that crossed the river was mostly gone, and it looked as if it had been that way for a very long time. The only parts that remained were the wooden handrails on either side of the river. The actual bridge, including any supporting structures in the river, had been swept away by the fast-flowing waters long ago.

'Well, there's no way we're going to get the caravans across the river,' said Milo.

'Maybe someone in the village has got a boat we can borrow?' suggested Jack.

'It's not going to be an easy journey,' said Hunk. 'That river is really fast. It's going to be hard to row against the current.'

'It's the only answer,' said Jack. 'Unless there's another way to get across.'

They drove the caravans back to the fork in the road, and then on to the small village. As they pulled the two caravans to a halt on the green, the villagers came out of their houses, expressions of curiosity clear on their faces.

'I guess they don't get many visitors here,' murmured Meenu.

'I'm not surprised,' grunted Robin.

The first to arrive was a large round man with a big moustache and a wide, welcoming smile.

'Good day!' he said, walking up to Big Rock and shaking the surprised troll by the hand. 'I'm the Mayor of Greengrass, our village. Welcome!'

Milo jumped down from the caravan and walked over to introduce himself.

'I'm Milo,' he said. Quickly, he introduced the others.

'We don't get many people coming here,' smiled a woman. 'I'm Mrs Best. It's lovely to have some new company!'

'Will you be staying long?' asked the Mayor.

'Actually, we're here on a mission,' said Jack. He pointed across the river at the castle high on the mountain. 'We have to get to Castle Dark. I'm guessing that's it on top of that mountain.'

At this, the smiles on the villagers' faces vanished, to be replaced by worried glances between them.

'I'm afraid that's not possible,' said the Mayor.

'The bridge is down,' said Mrs Best.

'Yes, we saw that,' said Jack. 'We wondered if there was another way across the river, or if anyone could lend us a boat.'

Again, the villagers exchanged anxious looks. Finally, the Mayor said: 'I'm afraid not.'

'But we need to get over there!' insisted Jack.

'Out of the question,' said Mrs Best firmly.

'Why?' asked Milo.

The villagers again looked at one another unhappily, then the Mayor announced: 'It's forbidden to set foot on Mount Doom, or to enter Castle Dark.'

'Forbidden by who?' asked Ava.

'Us!' blurted out the woman. 'The gates of Castle Dark have been shut these last ten years. It's the only way to keep the Horror locked in!'

# CHAPTER 5

'The Horror?' asked Jack, puzzled.

'The Horror is inside there,' nodded the Mayor. 'But if the gates are opened, it will escape and destroy us and everything around here!'

The gang exchanged puzzled glances.

'Lord Veto's message didn't say anything about a Horror,' murmured Jack to Milo. Aloud, he asked: 'What exactly is this Horror?'

The villagers shuddered, the fear clear in their faces.

'It's the most dangerous and deadly thing ever!' said the woman.

'But what does it *look* like?' insisted Jack.

Mrs Best shook her head.

'No one knows,' she said. 'No one's ever seen it.'

'But we know it's there,' said the Mayor. 'It's the curse of Mount Doom.'

'We were told ten years ago that a dreaded Horror had been locked inside the Castle,' said an older man. 'We were told, if we valued our lives, we must never ever go into Castle Dark, or let anyone else go into it. If anyone did, the Horror would be released.'

'That's why we destroyed the bridge,' said another man. 'So that no one could ever get into Castle Dark.'

Jack shook his head.

'Well, I'm sorry,' he said, 'but we have to. My grandfather's a prisoner in there, and I'm here to rescue him.'

The Mayor stared at Jack, shocked.

'That's impossible!' he said. 'No one's been in the castle for nearly ten years!'

'My grandfather's there,' said Jack. He produced the message and handed it to the Mayor. 'This is the message he sent me.'

The Mayor read it, then passed it to the other villagers, who all read it in turn before passing it back to Jack.

'I'm sorry,' said the Mayor firmly. 'We can't allow you to go to the castle.'

'If you go in there, you'll release the Horror,' said Mrs Best, equally firmly.

'Got to go there!' growled Big Rock, and he advanced towards the villagers, his huge fists clenched, making the villagers step back from him nervously.

'Wait, Big Rock!' burst out Jack. He stepped in front of the troll and said, 'These people are right. After all, they live here. And if they say that no one's been in Castle Dark for a long time, it must be true.' He looked at the message and then put it in his pocket. 'This message must be a mistake. Or a joke someone's playing on us.'

'Not a very funny joke,' snorted Robin.

'No, but there it is.' Jack smiled at the villagers. 'Well, it looks like we've come a long way for nothing.'

'Well . . . maybe not for nothing,' said one man warily. He walked up to Big Rock and said nervously, 'I am right, aren't I? You are Big Rock, the Wrestling Troll?'

Big Rock nodded.

'I knew it!' exclaimed the man in delight. 'My name's Bill Bungo. I saw you wrestle years ago at a tournament in the big city! It was one of the best things I ever saw in my life!'

At this, there were murmurings from the other villagers, with the words 'Big Rock the Wrestling Troll!' being said excitedly.

'Listen,' said the Mayor. 'I know this must be a disappointment to you, not being able to get where you were going . . . but it's a long journey back down through the mountains, and as you're here –'

'Will you wrestle for us, Big Rock?' interrupted Bill Bungo eagerly.

'An exhibition match,' added the Mayor. 'Bill here used to wrestle in the old days . . .'

'It would be the best thing that could happen to me,' said Bungo. 'It would be an honour for me to say I've been in the same ring as Big Rock the famous Wrestling Troll.'

'Not sure,' said Big Rock, frowning. 'Might hurt you.'

'No, you wouldn't, Big Rock,' said Jack quickly. 'Do it like you do when you and I are training. You never hurt me. Come on, Big Rock. After all, it's a long way back, so we're going to have to stay here overnight.'

'Please, Big Rock!' appealed Bungo.

Big Rock nodded.

'Okay,' he said. 'Me wrestle.'

A great cheer went up from the villagers.

'Fantastic!' exulted the Mayor. 'Brilliant!' He shook Big Rock firmly by the hand. 'This will go down in the history of Greengrass!' Then he turned to the villagers. 'Right! Let's go and get things ready! We have to make a ring. And find a costume for Bill!'

As the villagers hurried off to make their preparations, the others gathered around Jack, curious.

'You gave in very easily, Jack,' said Milo.

'Yes, do you really think that message was either a mistake or a joke?' asked Ava.

'Especially after some of us have hauled a very heavy caravan for two days up a mountain road!' said Robin sourly.

Jack shook his head.

'No. I think Lord Veto is in there, and I still aim to rescue him,' he said. 'But we've got a problem: how to get to Castle Dark without the villagers stopping us.'

'They don't stop us!' said Big Rock firmly. 'We strong. Me. Hunk. Masked Avenger.

And Thud. We beat them all!'

'That would be wrong,' said Jack. 'These people aren't villains. They're just ordinary people doing what's best to protect themselves. It wouldn't be right to attack them and hurt them.'

'So how do we get past them and get to Castle Dark?' asked Milo. 'They'll notice if we try to get across the river.'

'Not if they're all watching Big Rock wrestle,' said Jack. 'That's why I thought we should agree to it.' And he outlined his plan. 'While the villagers are busy watching Big Rock, Blaze flies me, the Masked Avenger and Hunk over the river to the other side.'

'What about me?' demanded Robin.

'You, Milo and Meenu stay here and watch Big Rock wrestle, otherwise the villagers will wonder where we all are and get suspicious,' said Jack.

Milo frowned, uncertainly.

'I don't know,' he said. 'You don't know what you're going into over there.'

'Ninjas,' said Hunk.

'And the Horror,' said Ava. 'Whatever that is.'

Jack forced a smile.

'Well, we knew it wasn't going to be easy!' he said.

# CHAPTER 6

A makeshift wrestling ring had been set up in a barn, with bales of straw and an assortment of chairs scattered around it for the audience to sit on. Night had fallen, and torches and candles had been set up high on the barn walls. The place was packed – the whole village had turned out. This wrestling match was the biggest thing that had happened in Greengrass for many years.

Jack and Hunk stood at the back of the barn, by the door, with Blaze. They were waiting for Princess Ava, who was in her caravan, putting on her Masked Avenger costume.

Big Rock was in the ring, wearing his wrestling outfit: a faded and very patched blue leotard with a picture of a mountaintop on the chest. In the opposite corner Bill Bungo bounced around excitedly, barely able to contain his joy at being in the same ring as his wrestling hero. His costume looked like a pair of swimming trunks with lots of different coloured spangles sewn on.

Milo, Meenu and Robin were at the front of the audience, and they cheered loudly as the Mayor entered the ring to announce the bout.

'That's good!' nodded Hunk. 'Nice loud cheering to keep everyone's attention on the wrestling ring.'

Jack felt a tap on his arm and looked around to see that the Masked Avenger had put her head through the doorway.

'Ready?' she whispered.

Jack nodded. He poked Hunk and Blaze, then the four slipped out of the barn.

'Okay,' said Jack. 'Let's go.'

They headed for the river and the remains of the broken bridge. Night was falling and they moved carefully to avoid tripping over on the rough ground in the dark. They reached the broken bridge and looked down at the river.

Even in the darkness, the fast-rushing waters showed white from the foam.

'Right,' said Jack. 'Here we go!'

Suddenly a voice called out, 'Stop!'

A group of eight villagers had appeared from behind some nearby rocks. They were holding sticks and pitchforks. At their head was Mrs Best.

'I knew you'd try this!' said Mrs Best. 'Well, we're not going to let you do it!'

'I have to,' said Jack. 'My grandfather's in there, and I have to rescue him.'

'If you go in there and release the Horror, you'll be putting our families at risk!'

'We'll make sure the Horror doesn't escape,' said Hunk. 'I promise you.'

'That's not good enough,' said the woman. 'Turn back now.'

'Sorry,' said Jack. 'We can't do that.'

'In that case, you force us to do this,' said Mrs Best. She turned to the villagers. 'Get them!'

The villagers advanced, their sticks and the sharp points of their pitchforks pointing menacingly towards them.

'We don't want to hurt them!' Hunk appealed to Jack.

'We won't,' said Jack.

He took the ring from his pocket and slipped it on his finger, and the next second, Thud, the massive Wrestling Troll, appeared, towering over the villagers. They stared up at this giant, their mouths open in shock and awe. Before they knew what was happening, Thud had bundled them all together, trapping them.

'Blaze, wrap them up in a web,' said Hunk.

There was a flash of light and the phoenix had turned into a large spider. The spider leapt on the villagers and began spinning a web, the strong, sticky thread gluing them together.

When Blaze had finished, the villagers were inside a neat parcel of spider's web that trapped their arms and legs and covered their mouths, gagging them.

Then Thud vanished as Jack took off the ring.

'We'll release you as soon as we return,' he promised. 'And we'll deal with the Horror. Okay, Blaze. Get us over the river.'

Another flash of light and the phoenix turned into a large dragon, which then picked up Jack.

The dragon lifted off and flew over the raging river, putting Jack down on the other side.

Blaze flew back across the river and returned with the Masked Avenger, and then, finally, with Hunk.

The four of them looked up at the ominous shape of Mount Doom directly ahead, with Castle Dark at the top. Seeing it in the darkness made it seem even more threatening.

'It's a long climb up to the castle,' commented the Masked Avenger.

'No problem,' said Blaze, who was still in his dragon form. 'I'll fly you up to the top, one at a time.'

'We'd better be careful,' said Hunk. 'We don't know what this Horror is that the villagers talked about. We don't know where it is. And the messenger pigeon said it saw ninjas inside the castle.'

'The villagers also said the castle gates hadn't been opened in ten years,' added the Masked Avenger.

'If that's true, how did the Voyadis get Lord

Veto inside?' asked Jack.

'It must have been the same way I'm going to get you in,' said Blaze. 'By flying you into the courtyard.'

'You mean the Voyadis might have some kind of dangerous flying creature hidden here?' said the Masked Avenger.

'Maybe that's the Horror . . .' suggested Hunk.

The Masked Avenger gave a shudder. 'This just gets worse!'

Blaze took hold of Jack in his dragon claws and sailed upwards with a flap of his powerful wings. Up they went, until they were high above the castle. Jack saw there was just one glow of light coming from a barred window at the top of the castle.

'That must be where Lord Veto and Warg are being held,' he said.

'There's nowhere up there to put you down,' said Blaze, so he swooped low and dropped Jack gently in the courtyard, and then flew off again.

Alone in the courtyard, Jack looked around, his eyes searching the darkness for any sign of movement. The trouble was, the Horror could be anything, and ninjas dressed from head to foot in black so they wouldn't easily be seen. Another problem with ninjas was that their movements were so swift and silent that no one really saw them move . . . until it was too late.

Jack heard a flapping of wings above him and then Blaze descended, dropping the Masked Avenger beside Jack before flying off again.

'Any sign of the ninjas?' whispered the Avenger.

'No,' Jack whispered back.

'What about the Horror?'

Jack shook his head. 'The trouble is, we don't know what we're looking for. We don't know what form it takes.'

There was another flap of wings, then Blaze delivered Hunk beside them before changing back into a phoenix.

Hunk looked about him. 'Any sign of the enemy?'

'No,' said Jack. 'But I know where Lord Veto and Warg are being kept.'

'Yes, I saw it,' said Hunk. 'That light at the top of the tower.'

'So, do we have a plan?' asked the Avenger.

'Yes,' said Jack. He took the ring from his pocket. 'I turn myself into Thud and go up to that room. That way, if I meet any ninjas, I'll be able to deal with them.'

'And we'll keep an eye on things down here,' nodded Hunk. 'Make sure nothing comes after you.'

'You sure you're going to be all right?' asked Jack, worried.

Hunk and the Masked Avenger nodded.

'We'll have Blaze with us,' said the Avenger. 'If anyone really bad turns up, Blaze can always turn into a fire-breathing dragon.'

'Unless the Horror *is* a fire-breathing dragon,' said Jack, still worried.

'We'll deal with that if it happens,' said Blaze.

'And if you run into trouble, Jack, just shout and we'll come running!' said the Avenger.

# CHAPTER 7

Jack slipped the ring on his finger, and then – in the form of giant Wrestling Troll Thud – he went to the doorway at the bottom of the tower. The door was locked and didn't look as if it had been opened for many years – rust and cobwebs were all around it.

Thud raised one huge foot and smashed it against the door, which cracked and splintered, then fell apart.

Thud entered the tower and let his sight adjust to the gloom. A circular staircase of stone steps led upwards. Carefully, Thud made his way up the stairs, aware all the time of possible attacks. None came. No ninjas appeared, no ghosts, no spectral forms, no

Horror. Finally, he reached the top, where the yellow glow of light came through the bars that were set into a small window in the door. He strode to the door and pushed at it, and to his surprise the door swung open.

Warily, Thud entered the room.

At first sight the room appeared to be empty, but then Thud saw that a small, thin old man with a long white beard was sitting on a bench in one corner.

'It's all right,' said the old man, getting up. 'You can turn back into your usual shape.'

Thud stared at the old man, at the long cloak he wore. Then he took the ring off and put it back into his pocket, and became Jack once more.

'Who are you?' asked Jack. 'Where are Lord Veto and Warg?'

'Ah yes,' nodded the man. 'Your grandfather and his faithful orc. Well, they're not here.'

'I can see that!' burst out Jack angrily. 'I asked you where they are. What have you done with them?'

'Me? I've done absolutely nothing with them,' said the man. 'I have no idea where they are.'

'But – but –' stammered Jack, bewildered.

'Ah, the messenger pigeon!' smiled the man. 'Yes, that was me. I had to get you to come here, and I thought the best way was to send you that message.'

'You mean it was a lie?'

'Of course!'

'But . . . the carrier pigeon said it saw Lord Veto here, and Warg, and ninjas!'

'Yes. I told it to say that. I thought the ninjas were a clever touch. I was sure you'd jump to the conclusion that the Voyadis were behind it, keeping your poor old grandfather locked up here.' He smiled and shook his head. 'But, instead, it was me.'

'But . . . why?'

'The ring, of course! The Royal Troll Ring.'

Jack shook his head.

'It's no use to you. It only works on a half-troll with royal blood.'

'Yes, I know that's how it works on you. But

turning a half-troll into a very enormous troll is only one of the things it does,' said the man. 'It has other properties that are much more valuable. Especially to a wizard.'

Jack looked at the man warily.

'You're a wizard?' he asked.

'Wazzo, at your service,' nodded the man, and he bowed, waving one hand towards Jack at the same time.

Jack felt a tugging at his feet, and he looked down to see that thick tree roots had sprouted from between the flagstones on the floor and were gripping his feet and ankles, and spreading upwards, coiling tightly around his legs and body.

Urgently, Jack plunged his hand towards his pocket, making a grab for the ring to slip it on again, but there was a sudden growth spurt from the plants and he found his arms pinned to his sides by the thick vines before he could reach it.

'Too slow. You should have put the ring back on more quickly, Jack,' said Wazzo.

'You won't get away with this!' stormed Jack. 'My friends are here. And he shouted as loud as he could, 'Help! Help!'

Immediately there was the sound of footsteps pounding up the stone stairs, then Hunk burst into the room, followed by the Avenger and Blaze.

'Watch out!' Jack shouted. 'He's a wizard!'

'We'll soon see about that!' yelled the Masked Avenger, and she rushed towards Wazzo, at the same time as Hunk launched himself into an attack and Blaze flapped his wings ready to swoop.

But the wizard calmly flicked his fingers, and the three of them froze: the Masked Avenger mid-run, Hunk on one leg, as if he was about to leap, and strangest of all was Blaze. The phoenix hovered in mid-air, wings outstretched, but perfectly still, as if being held up by invisible wires. They all looked like statues.

Wazzo clicked his fingers again and the roots brought Jack close to the wizard.

'Thank you, Jack,' he said. 'Now we can talk without any interference. After all, you're the one I want. The one with the ring.' He stepped forwards, dipped his fingers into Jack's pocket and took out the ring. 'Or rather, you *were* the one with the ring. Now it's mine.' He looked as if he was about to put it on his finger, but then he stopped. 'No, I think I'll wait a bit longer. Make it more special. And there are a few things I have to do first, before I put it on.'

'What things?' asked Jack, aware that the vines and tree roots holding him remained tight. Desperately, he tried to will himself to turn into Thud so he could break them, but it was no use.

'I have to make sure that the ring really will free me, and that the holding spell that keeps me prisoner here won't return once I break it.' He scowled. 'The wizard who cast it was really sneaky. He was capable of all sorts of dirty tricks!'

'A holding spell?' repeated Jack, puzzled.

'A troll wizard called Crumble put it on me!' said Wazzo, who now stopped smiling and looked vengeful. He leaned forwards and glared into Jack's face. 'I have been trapped here in this castle for nearly ten years, ever since I upset the Troll King; your father's father.'

'So you're the one the villagers call the Horror!'

Wazzo gave a scornful laugh.

'There is no such thing as the Horror! That was a story Crumble the troll wizard spread when he imprisoned me here!'

'Why did he do that?'

'Crumble wanted to make sure that no one would ever dare come near the castle and free me, so he invented the Horror to scare people away.'

'So this isn't anything to do with the Voyadis?' asked Jack.

'Of course not!' said Wazzo. 'Just because the

Voyadis *seem* to be involved in everything bad that goes on, it doesn't mean they are!' He looked at Jack with a cunning expression and asked: 'How much do you know about your parents?'

Jack stared at him, surprised by the question.

'I know that my father was a troll prince and my mother was Lord Veto's daughter, Leonora. They fell in love, but their fathers wanted to stop them getting married. So they ran away. Soon after I was born, Lord Veto traced them and caught up with them on a mountain top. Lord Veto had his Wrestling Orcs with him. There was a struggle, and my father fell off the mountain to his death. Lord Veto took his daughter and me back to Veto Castle. She died of a broken heart. He kept me as a slave in his kitchens until he kicked me out when I was ten years old.'

Wazzo nodded.

'Is that the story Lord Veto told you?' asked the wizard.

'I suppose you're going to tell me he lied!' snorted Jack. 'Well, that's nothing new. My grandfather is a cheat and a liar.'

'In this case, Lord Veto didn't know the whole story,' said Wazzo. 'What he told you was the truth, as far as he knew it. What he didn't know was that there was someone else in the Troll Kingdom who wanted to be king. His name was Moss and he was a cousin of your father's. He knew that Lord Veto had traced your father and mother to the mountain, and he paid me to do some magic, so that your father would fall off the cliff and die.'

Jack stared at Wazzo, stunned.

'So it was you who killed my father! Not Lord Veto!'

Wazzo gave an evil smile and nodded. 'I used my magic to make Lord Veto and his orcs think they'd done it.' Then he scowled, fierce anger showing in his eyes. 'Unfortunately, the Troll King found out about Moss's plan, and my part in it. He had Moss broken up into tiny bits of rock. My punishment was to be locked up in this castle and kept here by a holding spell so I could never leave. The Troll King wanted me to learn to hate this mountain. You see, Mount Doom is where your father died.'

'Here?' said Jack, shocked.

'Yes,' said Wazzo. He held up the ring. 'And the holding spell can only be broken by a wizard wearing this ring – your father's ring. But no one knew what had happened to it. And after the old Troll King died, no one knew where it might be. But then, a few months ago, I heard a rumour that you had found the ring.' His evil, smug smile returned to his face. 'I still have friends among the messenger pigeons. They keep me informed about the outside world.'

'You killed my father!' cried Jack angrily.

'It was nothing personal, it was a business transaction! I was to be paid a great deal of money for my work!' snapped back Wazzo. He looked lovingly at the ring in his hand. 'Ten years I've been trapped here, and now at last I can be free! And then I'll have my revenge!'

'On who?'

'On everyone!' shouted the wizard, his anger flashing. 'On Crumble, the Troll wizard who locked me up here. On the Troll King! But, as he's dead, you'll do in his place. On all those who helped you get here. On the villagers who've left me to rot all these years. On everybody!'

'What the villagers said is true,' said Jack. 'There really is a Horror. And it's you.'

Wazzo gave a nasty smile.

'Those people don't know the meaning of horror!' he cackled. 'When I'm free, I shall destroy them all! And, best of all, I shall kill you! That will be my final revenge against the Troll King! The death of the heir to the Troll throne! The end of the Troll Kings!'

'Wait!' Jack called desperately. 'You said you were going to wait until you'd made sure it was going to work!'

'I've changed my mind,' said Wazzo. 'I *know* this ring will free me. The longer I hold it, the more I can feel its power.'

As Wazzo held the ring poised over his finger, ready to slip it on, panic and rage boiled inside Jack. It was this man, this evil wizard, who'd actually killed his father. And he'd done it here! Well, he wasn't going to get away with it! Jack felt the familiar quartz film starting to cloud his eyes, felt his muscles beginning to creak and bulge, felt himself growing taller and bigger, and the vines that bound him struggling to keep hold . . .

'GRAAARRR!' he roared.

Through the film over his eyes, Thud saw Wazzo, unfazed, thrust his finger into the ring and slide it on.

*BOOOMMM!!!!*

There was a flash of light that blinded Thud. When he could see again, where Wazzo had stood there was now just a heap of charred smouldering ash, with the ring lying on top. The tree roots and vines that had held Jack prisoner withered and shrank, falling to the floor and decaying before his eyes. At the same time, the Masked Avenger, Hunk and Blaze came back to life.

'What happened?' asked the Avenger, looking dazed.

Thud, shrinking back down to the smaller figure of Jack, looked at the small heap of smouldering ash.

'It's a long story,' he said.

# CHAPTER 8

The Mayor of Greengrass looked apologetically at Jack.

'I'm sorry for the way we treated you –' he began.

'There's no need to apologise,' Jack interrupted him. 'You only did what you thought was best to protect your community. We're the ones who should apologise for tying up some of your people the way we did.'

'Yes, you should apologise,' snapped Mrs Best. 'That sticky spidery stuff isn't easy to get off clothes!'

'I've got some cleaner at home that's good for getting off spider stuff,' said Meenu. 'I'll send you some as soon as we get back to Weevil.'

Mrs Best looked as if she was about to make another angry retort, then she stopped.

'You got rid of the Horror,' she said. 'That's the main thing. You saved us.'

'There was no Horror, just a very angry wizard,' said Ava.

'He was Horror enough,' said Jack, shuddering at the memory of the tree roots and vines. 'And he would have been a true Horror if he'd got out.'

'The point is, we can now go away occasionally, on holidays and things,' said the Mayor.

'You see, we've been afraid to leave the village in case anyone turned up and tried to get into the Castle,' added Mrs Best. 'The only one who's ever left is Bill Bungo, when he went to the city for a week.'

'When I saw Big Rock wrestle!' beamed Bill Bungo. And he shook his head in wonder. 'To think, I actually beat the famous Big Rock in a wrestling match!'

'Good wrestling,' smiled Big Rock, and he shook Bill Bungo's hand.

As they made their way back to the caravans, Milo scowled at Big Rock: 'There was no need to let him win!'

'You said –'

'We said not to hurt him! I never said let him win!'

'It make him happy,' said Big Rock.

'Yes, it did,' said Hunk. 'I thought that was a really nice thing to do.'

Jack looked across at Mount Doom on the other side of the river. So that was where his father had died. Killed by Wazzo, the evil wizard.

*I have to let Lord Veto know,* he promised himself. *He didn't kill my father . . . I knew he couldn't be as completely evil as everyone thinks. But I'll still never forgive him for what he did to my mother . . .*

He was aware that Princess Ava had arrived next to him.

'That wizard,' she said quietly. 'Why did he explode?'

'It was the ring,' said Jack. 'Crumble, the Troll wizard, must have put a spell on it so that if Wazzo ever put it on, it would kill him.' He shook his head. 'The Troll King must have hated him a great deal for killing my father. It was the ultimate revenge. Lock Wazzo up and tell him that if he could get hold of the ring he'd be able to escape. Knowing he'd suffer there for years and years before he could find it – if ever. And when he did . . . *bang!* The end.'

'At least the Voyadis aren't after you, and you now know that Lord Veto didn't kill your father,' said Ava.

'I know, but he *was* responsible for the death of my mother,' sighed Jack. 'He locked her up so she died of a broken heart.'

Jack made for his caravan, his head bowed, where Milo had already climbed onto the driving seat. Princess Ava hesitated, as if she was about to go after him and say something sympathetic. Then she shrugged and joined Meenu, who was waiting on the driving seat of their caravan.

'Everything all right?' asked Meenu.

'I suppose so,' said Ava. She sighed. 'I was going to try to cheer him up, but I don't think anything I can say will help him at this moment.' She sighed again, even more deeply. 'I don't think Jack's ever going to be happy.'

'He will be one day,' said Meenu. She smiled. 'When he grows up and meets the right girl.'

'He's a prince,' Ava reminded Meenu. 'They can't have just any old girlfriend.'

'No, I know,' said Meenu. And she gave a sly smile. 'It has to be someone royal. Like a princess.'

Ava gave Meenu an indignant look.

'What are you suggesting?' she demanded.

'Well, he's a prince and you're a princess,' said Meenu. 'And it's obvious you both like one another very much . . .'

'It is NOT obvious!' said Ava. 'And besides, I'm not interested! I'm a champion wrestler. I don't need a boyfriend! Right?'

'Right,' nodded Meenu.

Princess Ava flicked the reins. She was still scowling at Meenu's suggestion, but Meenu saw that a red flush was starting to spread up the Princess's face. Was Ava . . . blushing?

'Giddyup,' said Ava quickly, and their horse moved forwards to follow Jack and Milo's caravan.

# THE FINAL SHOWDOWN

# CHAPTER 1

CRASH!!

The whole arena seemed to vibrate as the two huge Wrestling Trolls hurled themselves at one another and came to a rock-crunching collision in the centre of the ring before bouncing off again.

It had been a whole month since the gang had left Mount Doom, and now they were back on the wrestling circuit. This tournament was in a village called Pummel, not far from their home country, and this bout was between Big Rock and a troll called Forest. Forest was so called because not only was he made of rock and quartz, but plants and shrubs sprouted from the cracks in his rocky skin and the top of his head, giving him what looked like a riot of hair in different colours.

The match was even so far: one pinfall each to Big Rock and Forest. 'Forest is tough,' murmured Jack nervously as the plant-covered troll once again threw himself at Big Rock, this time sending Big Rock staggering backwards.

'Big Rock's fought tougher,' replied Milo confidently.

Then he winced as Forest grabbed hold of Big Rock by one arm and swung him hard, round and round, before releasing him flying into the corner post.

THUMP!

Big Rock slid down the post into a heap.

'You were saying?' asked Jack.

'He's lulling Forest into a false sense of security,' said Milo, although this time he didn't sound as confident.

As Big Rock struggled to his feet, Forest launched another attack, this one taking the form of a two-footed drop kick aimed at Big Rock's head.

Just in time, Big Rock moved his head to one side, but Forest's boots hit him in the shoulder and sent him spinning wildly.

BANG!

Another kick from Forest connected with Big Rock's chest, and he crashed through the ropes and smashed into the ground outside the ring.

'Get up, Big Rock!' yelled Jack desperately, as the referee began the count for the knockout: 'One. Two. Three. Four . . .'

In the ring, Forest was already jumping around, celebrating, waving at his cheering supporters, while Big Rock pushed himself to his feet and stood, swaying unsteadily.

'Five. Six. Seven . . .'

Forest came to the ropes and leaned over them, looking down at Big Rock in triumph.

'Eight,' counted the referee.

'So, Big Rock –' grinned Forest.

That was as far as he got. Big Rock reached up, grabbed hold of a small bush hanging down from Forest's head and jerked the troll out of the ring, then letting go of Forest's hair at the same time as diving through the ropes back into the ring.

Forest let out a roar of anger and frustration, and shot back into the ring as the referee began his count against him. As Forest hurled himself at Big Rock, both of his big hands reaching out, Big Rock ducked and let Forest sail over him. Forest hit the ropes, which bounced him back into the centre of the ring, where he crashed down.

Forest pushed himself to his knees, shaking his head, but before he could get up, Big Rock had done a backwards somersault from the side of the ring and landed directly on top of Forest, flattening him.

Dazed, Forest lay on his back with Big Rock on top of him, pinning his shoulders to the canvas.

'One!' shouted the referee. 'Two! Three!'

The crowd in the arena went wild as Big Rock

got to his feet and then held out his hand to help Forest up.

'Yes!' cried Jack. 'Fantastic! What a victory!'

'Good match,' said Forest.

As the two trolls shook hands, the referee tried shouting to announce that Big Rock was the winner, but he couldn't make himself heard above the excited yells of the audience.

Afterwards, Jack, Milo and Big Rock joined Robin and Blaze outside.

'Big Rock won!' Jack told them.

'The outcome was never in doubt,' said the old horse confidently.

'It was if you were watching the match,' said Jack. 'Wasn't it close, Milo?'

Milo shook his head.

'No,' he said smugly. 'I always knew Big Rock was going to win.'

'Hello,' said Blaze suddenly. 'It looks like an old friend of ours is here.'

They followed the phoenix's gaze and saw the figure of Dunk the Dangerous Orc hurrying towards them.

'Dunk!' cried Jack. 'We didn't know you were here! Did you see the bout? Wasn't Big Rock great? That fantastic back-flip at the end to get to that final pinfall!'

'I didn't see it,' admitted Dunk. 'I've only just got here.'

'Shame,' said Big Rock. 'Good match.'

'You look worried, Dunk,' said Milo. 'What's the matter?'

'That's why I've come to find you,' said Dunk. 'Terrible things are happening at Veto Castle. You know the Voyadis took it from Lord Veto in settlement for his debts to them. Well, now they have put a troll called Massive in charge of the whole estate, with an army of trolls, and he's declared it a "Troll Homeland", with himself as King of the Trolls.'

'He not King of Trolls,' snorted Big Rock. 'Jack true king!'

'I don't want to be a king, Big Rock,' said Jack. 'I keep telling everyone that. I only want to be part of Waldo's Wrestling Trolls, just like we are now.'

'And anyway, it's nice for trolls to have a place of their own,' said Milo. 'Somewhere they can call home.'

'Yes, but it's not nice for everyone else,' said Dunk. 'Massive has called for all Trolls to join him there, and he's told the orcs who live there that they're being kicked out. He's got papers to show that he owns the whole Veto estate. Not just Veto Castle, but all the villages and houses for miles and miles around. Some orcs have been living on this land for generations. Okay, there have been some disagreements between trolls and orcs, but we've all lived together for as long as anyone can remember. And now the orcs are being turned out of their houses, and they've got nowhere to go.'

'That wrong,' said Big Rock.

'Isn't there a Troll Council or something that can tell Massive he's doing the wrong thing and make him stop?' asked Milo.

'No Troll Council,' said Big Rock. 'Only Troll King could give orders. And when last Troll King died, that was the end.' He looked at Jack.

'But now Jack Troll King, he can tell Massive to stop.'

'I'm not the Troll King,' insisted Jack.

'You've got the Royal Troll Ring,' said Dunk. 'Your father was the heir to the Troll throne. That makes you the next in line.' He looked hopefully at Jack and asked: 'Couldn't you have a word with Massive? He might listen to you. It's terrible what he's doing to these orcs. Children are being dumped outside the estate, with nowhere to go.'

'But if the Voyadis are behind it, doesn't someone need to appeal to them to stop Massive?'

'The Voyadis! Huh!' snorted Dunk. 'They're not exactly easy to pin down. But I thought if Jack could persuade Massive to do the right thing, that would give us leverage with the Voyadis.'

'Well, I can try,' said Jack doubtfully.

'Amazing!' said Robin. 'I never thought I'd see the day when one of us would be standing up for orcs!'

'Dunk an orc, and he good,' said Big Rock. 'Not all orcs bad!'

'Thank you, Big Rock,' said Dunk. He gave Jack a worried look. 'If you aren't able to persuade Massive, Jack, it could be the end for all orcs. We'll be driven out of our homes, and I don't know where we'll go!'

# CHAPTER 2

The battered old caravan with WWT on the side – for Waldo's Wrestling Trolls – found it harder and harder to roll onwards the nearer it got to Veto Castle, because of the large numbers of orcs leaving the castle grounds. Most of them seemed to be orc families, pulling their belongings on carts.

'Traffic jam,' muttered Robin, pulling to a halt.

'I'll go and see how bad it is,' said Blaze, and the phoenix lifted up into the air and flew towards the gateway of the castle and over the walls. He returned shortly afterwards.

'It looks like every orc for miles around is leaving,' he said. 'The gateway is jammed, but I saw some troll soldiers heading for it. I guess someone saw our caravan coming.'

As he said that, two large trolls armed with clubs emerged from the crowd and ordered the orcs to get out of the road.

'Make way for trolls!' they commanded.

The orcs pushed their carts to one side, clearing the entrance, and Robin pulled the old caravan through the gateway and into the grounds.

'This is horrible,' Jack whispered to Milo as they sat together on the driving seat.

'Yes,' nodded Milo. 'It's lucky Dunk's inside the caravan or I'm pretty sure those troll guards would have stopped him coming in.'

Big Rock trotted alongside the caravan, with Blaze flying overhead.

'Lots of trolls,' said Big Rock. He smiled. 'Good.'

'Yes, but not good for the orcs,' said Jack.

The caravan rolled past areas where some trolls were digging up earth and making themselves homes. Other trolls were taking over empty houses and moving their furniture in.

There was movement from inside the caravan,

and Dunk pushed his way between Jack and Milo.

'What's going on?' he asked, settling himself on the driving seat.

'I wouldn't spend too long outside the caravan, if I were you,' advised Robin. 'It looks as if orcs aren't very popular here.'

'Oh no!' exclaimed Dunk, shocked. He pointed to where an orc woman and two small orc children were being forced out of a cottage by a gang of trolls and pushed towards a large cart. The cart was already almost filled with orc women and children. 'That's my Aunt Roz and my cousins, Beck and Bock!' said Dunk.

He suddenly jumped down from the caravan and ran towards the cart, shouting, 'Stop! Stop! You can't do this! They've lived here all their lives! It's wrong!'

'Uh-oh,' groaned Robin, pulling to a halt. 'I think we're going to be in trouble!'

The huge troll who had been lifting up the little orc girl dumped her in the cart and turned to glare at Dunk.

'Shut up!' he snarled. 'We don't listen to what orcs say!'

With that, the troll grabbed the little boy orc and threw him in the cart as well.

Big Rock growled and hurried over to face the troll.

'Me a troll!' he snapped. 'I say this wrong!'

The troll stared at Big Rock, stunned, then he scowled.

'A troll siding with orcs against trolls!' he snarled. 'That's treason!'

'No, it right,' said Big Rock.

With that, Big Rock strode to the cart and lifted the two orc children out of it, one in each hand, and put them down on the ground.

'There!' said Big Rock. 'You go back home.' He turned to the orc woman, who was looking on nervously. 'You go home too.'

'No!' shouted the troll. 'This is troll land now! No orcs allowed!'

'Yes, I definitely think we're in trouble,' muttered Robin.

Jack and Milo climbed down from the driving seat and hurried to where Big Rock and Dunk were arguing with the big troll, just in time to hear the troll calling out: 'Guards! Guards!'

His cries brought a troop of twenty big trolls hurrying over. They were all armed with clubs.

'What's going on?' demanded the Troll Captain.

'This troll and this orc are stopping us kicking these orcs out.'

The Troll Captain stared at Big Rock, shocked.

'A troll siding with orcs!' he exclaimed.

'That's what I said,' nodded the troll. 'It's treason!'

'It certainly is!' said the Captain. 'Right! You're both under arrest!' He turned to the guards and ordered, 'Take them to Massive!'

'You can't do that!' protested Jack. 'Don't you know who this is? He's Big Rock, the Champion Troll Wrestler!'

The Captain scowled.

'Yes, I know who he is,' he said. 'And I never thought I'd see the day when a troll as famous as Big Rock would choose to side with our enemies.'

'Orcs aren't your enemies!' protested Jack.

'Yes, they are!' snapped back the Captain. 'And we're getting rid of them! There'll be no orcs in this Troll Homeland!'

'Look,' began Milo, appealing to the Captain, 'I know you have your orders. But Big Rock is a famous troll. Everyone loves him!'

'I don't care how famous he is; if he sides with orcs, he's a traitor! And you lot are lucky I don't arrest you as well!'

'On what charge?' demanded Jack indignantly.

'For not being trolls,' said the Captain. 'Now get off this land!' He turned to the guards who were pointing their clubs at Big Rock and Dunk and repeated his order: 'Take them to Massive!'

'Wait!' burst out Milo. 'We have to go with them! We're their lawyers! If they're being charged, we have the right to defend them at their trial!'

The Trolls looked at Milo and the others with puzzled frowns.

'You're *all* lawyers?' asked the Captain.

'Yes,' said Milo.

'The horse and the phoenix as well?'

'Of course,' said Robin.

'The horse is the brains behind the team,' said Blaze.

The Troll Captain regarded them suspiciously.

'Okay,' he said. 'You can all come. But if there are any tricks, you'll all be in serious trouble!'

# CHAPTER 3

Jack, Milo, Robin and Blaze followed as the troll guards escorted Big Rock and Dunk through the big main entrance of Veto Castle, and then along the dark wooden-walled corridors to the Big Hall. A huge throne painted with gold had been set up in the middle of the Big Hall, and a very large troll sat on it, a gold crown on his head. Yes, he certainly lived up to his name of Massive, thought Jack. The throne was flanked by troll guards armed with clubs. And almost hidden behind the throne were three hooded figures dressed from head to foot in black.

'Ninjas,' Jack whispered to Milo.

'I see them,' Milo whispered back. 'The Voyadis must be behind this.'

Massive looked at them questioningly as they were marched into his presence, and his lips curled in distaste when he spotted Dunk.

'An orc!' he exploded at the troll guard who had brought them. 'You dare to bring an orc into my presence!'

Hastily the troll explained what had happened, and how he'd placed Big Rock and Dunk under arrest. But Massive seemed to have stopped listening to the guard. Instead, he was concentrating his attention on Jack.

'Well, well!' he said. 'So, it's Jack, Lord Veto's former kitchen boy, come back home.'

Immediately, Jack was on his guard. How did this troll know who he was? He was about to ask that question, when Massive leaned forwards and demanded, 'Have you got the ring on you?'

'What ring?' asked Jack.

Massive gave a derisive laugh.

'Oh, come on!' he snorted. 'Everyone knows all about the Royal Troll Ring!' He shook his head. 'It's not yours, you know. By rights, it belongs to the King of the Trolls. And that's me.'

'It not you!' barked Big Rock. 'Jack King of Trolls!'

'How can he be? He's a human!' shouted Massive.

'He half-troll!' shouted back Big Rock. 'His father Prince of Trolls!'

'Shut up!' shouted back Massive. 'I'm not going to be told what's right and wrong by a traitor!'

'Big Rock is no traitor,' said Jack. 'He was only doing what he thought was right: defending a woman and two small children against bullies who were turning them out of their home.'

'They were orcs!' spat Massive. 'Orcs have no place in the Troll Homeland!' Angrily, he pointed an accusing finger at Big Rock. 'As King of Troll-Land, I find you guilty of treason. And the punishment for treason is death! So, Big Rock, you will be locked up in a cell and then executed just as soon as I've decided what sort of execution to use. And the same goes for your orc friend!' And he glared at Dunk. 'Lock them up!'

'Wait a minute!' protested Milo. 'You can't do that! People are supposed to have a proper trial!'

'These are their lawyers, Your Majesty,' said the Troll Captain. He pointed at the old horse. 'He's the brains of the team.'

'And I see you have a phoenix!' grinned Massive. Suddenly, before the others realised what was happening, Massive had produced a large metal net on a long pole from its hiding place behind his throne and dropped the net over Blaze, trapping him.

Immediately, Blaze let out a blaze of light, and the others watched, wondering what the phoenix was going to turn into. But when the light cleared, there was Blaze looking the same as ever.

Massive let out a chuckle.

'A magic net!' he boasted. 'I knew you'd be bringing a phoenix, so I was ready.' He looked at Robin and laughed. 'If you really are the brains of this outfit you should have thought of that!'

'I've never thought of trolls as sneaky before,' retorted the old horse. 'But then, I've never met a troll as sneaky and dishonest as you.'

'Don't you dare talk to His Majesty like that!' stormed the Troll Captain.

'The Voyadis must have told him about Blaze,' muttered Milo to Jack. 'I bet they've told him everything about us.'

Massive smirked at them.

'There is a way to save their lives.' He held out his hand towards Jack. 'Give me the ring.'

Jack shook his head.

'No,' he said. 'That's my ring.'

'It's the ring of the Troll King!' snarled Massive. He glared at Jack. 'That's what you're after, isn't it. You want to be King of the Trolls!'

'Absolutely not!' denied Jack. 'I'm keeping it because it was left to me by my mother. It was all she had of my father's.'

Massive stood up and advanced angrily on Jack.

'And I say you're keeping it because you want to be the Troll King!' he repeated, even more furious.

'No!' Jack shook his head. 'I don't want that kind of power. All I want is for everyone to live together happily: trolls, orcs, goblins, elves, humans – everybody!'

'And horses!' put in Robin.

'He did say "everybody",' Milo whispered to the old horse.

'Yes, but he didn't say horses specifically,' complained Robin. 'He named trolls and orcs and goblins and –'

'Shut up!' shouted Massive.

'Why are you doing this?' appealed Jack. 'You're a troll. Trolls are supposed to be the good guys!'

'And it's because we've been the good guys that we've let orcs walk all over us!' retorted Massive.

'But the orcs you're kicking out aren't bad!' protested Jack. 'They're kids, little orcs and their mums!'

Massive shook his head. 'And one day those little orcs will grow up to be big orcs, and they'll be our enemies. Well, I'm stopping that before it happens.' A sneaky smile spread over the big troll's face, and he said, 'There is another way you can save your treacherous friend and his orc pal.'

'What?' asked Jack.

'Wrestle me.'

'Wrestle you?' echoed Jack in surprise.

Massive nodded.

'If you win, I let Big Rock and the orc go. I'll also stand down as Troll King and leave, and you can become Troll King.'

'What happens if you win?' asked Milo.

'If I win, they die and I get the ring. Oh, and Jack dies as well, for treason.'

'How can he be accused of treason?' demanded Robin.

'Because he refused to give me the ring. And I'm Troll King. And he is half-troll'

'That's nonsense!' snorted Milo.

'I'll do it!' burst out Jack.

The others turned to look at him.

'No!' said Big Rock. 'You proper king already, Jack! You not wrestle for it!'

'That's more treason!' burst out Massive. 'Take them to the cells!'

As the guards took Big Rock and Dunk away, Jack squared up to Massive.

'I mean it,' he said. 'I'll wrestle you on those terms.'

'Good,' smiled Massive. 'We'll hold the match in Lord Veto's old wrestling arena here at the castle, in two hours. That'll give us time to warm up and get ready.'

Milo moved forwards to lift up the net to take Blaze with them, but Massive's hand moved fast, stopping him.

'No you don't!' he growled. 'The phoenix stays here, under the net. I don't want it getting up to any of those sneaky phoenix tricks, like changing shape and turning into me.'

'I don't think I'd want to turn into you,' said Blaze scornfully. 'Being you would make me feel sick.'

'Shut up!' snarled Massive. 'Or else you'll find yourself on the menu to celebrate my coronation: roast phoenix and chips!'

# CHAPTER 4

As they left Veto Castle, they saw that a familiar caravan had pulled up outside, and Princess Ava, Meenu and Hunk were climbing down from it.

'Ava!' called Jack delightedly. 'What brings you here?'

'I'm guessing the same thing that brought you,' said Ava. 'We were taking part in a tournament nearby when we heard what was going on with Massive.' She shook her head. 'It's awful!'

'Where's Big Rock?' asked Hunk, looking around, worried. 'Is it true what they say? That he's been arrested? Him and Dunk the Orc?'

'I'm afraid so,' said Milo.

'We heard the guards saying just now that you're going to wrestle Massive, Jack. Is that true?' asked Meenu.

'Yes,' nodded Jack.

'You idiots!' burst out Ava. 'How can you be so stupid!'

Jack and Milo looked at her, shocked.

'Now wait a moment,' Milo protested. 'Jack's doing it to save the lives of Big Rock and Dunk.'

'Yes. And I'm also doing it to stop Massive from getting control of this place,' added Jack.

'It's not Massive who's behind this!' said Ava. 'Do you really think a troll could come up with something as sneakily clever as this?'

'Actually, some of us are quite clever,' put in Hunk, a little upset.

'Clever, yes, but not sneaky!' said Ava quickly, realising she'd hurt Hunk's feelings. 'Massive didn't think this plan up on his own. It's the Voyadis who are behind it: they were the ones who took Lord Veto's castle and lands. The Voyadis are using Massive to start a war between trolls and orcs, and from there they will take over the areas and estates bordering on Veto Castle's lands, and spread outwards. But first, they have to get rid of the true heir to the Troll Kingdom – Jack!'

Jack, Milo and the others looked uncomfortable.

'That seems a bit extreme, even for the Voyadis,' said Milo doubtfully.

'Oh yes?' said Ava sarcastically. 'Where's Blaze?'

'He's been taken prisoner by Massive,' said Robin.

'Let me guess – in a metal net that works by magic?' asked Ava.

'Er . . . yes,' said Jack. 'How did you know?'

'Because the Voyadis have been working on some kind of magic net that controls phoenixes.'

'We said the Voyadis were involved somehow – we saw their ninjas in the castle,' said Robin. 'We knew they were dangerous, but this is something really clever!'

'And horrible!' said Meenu.

'Er . . . of course,' said Robin hastily. 'When I said "clever", I really meant "horrible". Very bad.'

'It doesn't matter,' said Jack. 'I've got the ring. When I wrestle Massive, I'll put on the ring and turn into Thud. I'll beat him. It's simple.'

'Where is the ring?' asked Ava.

'In my pocket,' said Jack. 'I keep it safe there.'

He patted his pocket and then stopped, a worried look crossing his face.

'Well?' demanded Ava.

Jack patted his pocket again, his expression getting more worried. Then he put his hand in his pocket.

'It must be in another pocket,' he said.

Frantically, he began searching through his other pockets. The others watched him, with anxious looks on their faces.

'It's gone, hasn't it?' said Ava.

'I must have dropped it,' said Jack.

'Or someone took it,' said Ava.

'Who?' asked Milo.

Ava shook her head.

'You lot really are stupid, aren't you?' she said, exasperated. 'The Voyadis, of course! The Voyadis had someone in that room who picked your pocket!'

'Those ninjas!' exclaimed Milo. 'They're sneaky and move so fast, I bet they pickpocketed it from you!'

'But I don't understand it,' said Jack, bewildered. 'You're saying that Massive has

already got the ring because he stole it from me?'

'Yes,' nodded Ava.

'So why did he suggest wrestling me for it, if he's already got it?'

'What were the terms you agreed?'

'If I win, he lets Big Rock and Dunk go. And he stands down as Troll King and leaves.'

'And if he wins?'

'He gets the ring. And Big Rock, Dunk and I die.'

'Exactly!' said Ava. 'That's what this is all about! He's going to kill Jack and put an end to his claim to the troll throne!'

Jack looked puzzled.

'But if that's his plan, why doesn't he kill me now? Why go through this stuff about a wrestling match?'

'To make it look legal,' said Milo. 'You're the heir to the troll throne. If he beats you in a wrestling match it makes his claim to the throne much stronger.'

'He might even be planning to kill Jack during the match,' said Ava, worried.

'So don't wrestle him!' said Milo. 'That'll put a stop to his plan!'

'No it won't,' said Robin sadly. 'If Jack refuses to wrestle, it'll be counted as him having given in. Massive will win.'

'And if Jack wrestles Massive without the ring to help him turn into Thud, Massive will win the match. Either way, Massive wins.'

'Maybe I'll turn into Thud during the bout?' suggested Jack hopefully.

The others looked at him doubtfully.

'It doesn't happen that often,' pointed out Milo. 'And without the ring, you can't make it happen for sure.'

Robin sighed.

'Looks like you're going to die, Jack,' he said.

# CHAPTER 5

'No!' burst out Ava. 'We're not going to let that happen!'

'How will we stop it?' asked Robin.

'We find the ring!'

'That is brilliant!' said Hunk admiringly. 'Why didn't we think of that?'

'Because you're all stu—' began Ava, then she changed it abruptly to '– stupendously nice people. You need to be sneaky to beat the Voyadis.'

Suddenly a frown crossed over Meenu's face.

'Talking of sneaky,' she murmured, 'I might be wrong, but I think someone very sneaky has just arrived.'

The others turned to look in the same direction as Meenu and saw two figures dressed completely in black from head to foot shuffling towards them.

'Ninjas!' exclaimed Milo, shocked.

'I don't think so,' said Meenu. 'These two are moving too slowly to be ninjas. And take a look at their feet.'

They did. One of the figures was wearing expensive-looking boots, the other had claws poking out from beneath the long black cloak.

'It can't be!' exclaimed Jack. 'It's Lord Veto and Warg!'

'Shush!' said one of the black-clad pair as they hurried towards the group. 'How did you know it was us?'

'The boots and the claws,' said Jack.

'Drat!' grimaced Lord Veto, throwing back his hood. 'This is your fault, Warg! I told you we should have had better disguises!'

'Why are you in disguise anyway?' asked Milo.

'Because there is danger for us here,' said

Lord Veto. 'This place is full of trolls in the pay of the Voyadis. Warg here is an orc. That puts him in danger from the trolls. I am Lord Veto, and naturally the Voyadis are jealous of my superior brain. And also, well, we haven't been on the best of terms since I owed them money and they took my castle . . .'

'So why are you here?' demanded Jack.

'I came as soon as I heard what had happened to my beloved grandson! Lured into a wrestling match with Massive, one that he will lose, and then he'll be killed.'

'How did you know about that?' asked Jack.

'It's only just been agreed!'

'I bet he's been hanging about here for ages, trying to work out how to get the castle back,' said Ava. 'I bet he overheard what Massive said!'

'And when he saw Jack he thought he'd try to rope him in to help him,' added Meenu.

'And why shouldn't I!' burst out Veto. 'This place is my family home. *Our* family home!' He looked appealingly at Jack. 'Just think about it, Jack. You are the true heir to the troll throne. I am your grandfather! Together, as a family, we can be wealthy and powerful!'

'Ha!' snorted Jack scornfully. 'I should have known – you're not concerned about me. You just want your precious money and power back.'

'Actually, Jack, he could be useful,' said Ava thoughtfully.

'But he's sneaky! And dishonest!' burst out Jack.

'Exactly,' nodded Ava, 'and if we're going to get the ring back and beat the Voyadis we need someone as sneaky as Lord Veto on our side.'

'Thank you, Your Highness,' said Lord Veto. Then he frowned. 'You mean the Voyadis have got hold of the ring already?'

'Yes,' said Milo. 'They pickpocketed it from him.'

'They're cleverer than I thought!' scowled Lord Veto. He looked around. 'Where are the others? That big troll wrestler, and that phoenix?'

'Big Rock is in the cells with Dunk the Orc,' said Milo.

'And Blaze is trapped inside a magic net in the castle,' said Robin.

'Right,' said Lord Veto, thinking hard. 'This is what we do . . .'

'Wait a minute!' snapped Jack. 'You're not in charge! You don't give the orders!'

'Very true,' nodded Veto. 'But if I were, I'd suggest that we need to split into groups – one to free Big Rock and Dunk from the cells; one to rescue Blaze; and one to search this place to find the ring.'

'Yes,' nodded Ava. 'That makes sense.'

'There is a secret tunnel that goes to the cells,' said Lord Veto.

'Yes, we've been in it before – and we didn't like it much,' said Ava. 'There are giant rats and spiders in there, and it floods!'

'Not that one,' said Veto. 'This is another one. Warg knows where it is.'

'How many secret tunnels are there in this place?' asked Robin.

'Lots,' said Lord Veto. 'The Veto family has always made sure it has lots of ways to escape if danger threatens. So, Warg, I suggest you use that tunnel to rescue Big Rock.'

'Yes, my Lord,' nodded the orc.

'I'll go with him,' said Hunk.

'Me too,' said Milo.

'Good. Next, we need to search for the ring,' said Lord Veto. 'And for that we need someone who knows the inside of the castle like the back of his hand.'

'Well, if you're going to do that, I'm staying with you!' said Meenu firmly.

'I suppose that leaves me to rescue Blaze,' said Robin.

'You won't be able to do it on your own,' said Jack. 'I'll come with you.'

'But you have to get ready for the wrestling match,' Milo told him.

'I can do both,' Jack assured him.

'I'll go with Meenu and Lord Veto to find the ring,' said Ava.

'Er, actually, Princess . . .' began Meenu carefully. 'It might be better if you get your *friend* to come with us instead.'

Princess Ava frowned.

'My friend?' she repeated.

'The Masked Avenger,' nodded Meenu. And she winked.

*Of course!* thought Ava. Her friends knew that the Masked Avenger was actually Princess Ava in disguise, but no one else did. And that included Lord Veto.

'I think that's a good idea, if I may say so, Your Highness,' nodded Lord Veto. 'We may run into danger, and a wrestler like the Masked

Avenger may be able to handle it. But you are a princess, a royal person, and not used to rough stuff.'

'Yes, good thinking,' nodded Ava. 'I'll go and get the Masked Avenger and tell her what she has to do.'

With that, she hurried off.

Hunk frowned, puzzled.

'But I thought that Princess Ava was –' he began. 'Ow!' he finished as Robin trod on his foot.

'Sorry,' said Robin. 'Was that your foot?'

'I was just saying that I thought –' said Hunk.

'Don't think,' said Robin. 'It's bad for you.'

'There's no time to chat!' yelled Meenu. 'The match starts in just over an hour – let's go!'

And the gang began to split up into their groups. Lord Veto was just about to hurry after Meenu when Jack stopped him.

'There's something you need to know,' he said. 'You and your orcs didn't kill my father. An evil wizard called Wazzo did. He used magic to make you think you'd done it.'

Lord Veto's face lit up with delight.

'Then I am innocent!' he cried with relief.

'Of that,' said Jack. 'But not of what happened to my mother.'

Lord Veto looked uncomfortable.

'That wasn't my fault,' he protested. 'She did it to herself. She refused to eat!'

'Because of the way *you* treated her,' retorted Jack. 'I will never forgive you.'

With that, Jack turned and hurried away to join Robin.

'You will one day, grandson . . .' muttered Lord Veto to himself.

# CHAPTER 6

Lord Veto paced impatiently outside Princess Ava's caravan.

'The Masked Avenger's taking her time!' he snapped at Meenu.

'She has to put her costume on,' said Meenu.

'I suppose so,' Veto grumbled. He shot a glance at Meenu. 'Do *you* know her real identity?'

'Even if I did, I wouldn't tell you,' said Meenu.

'I'd be prepared to pay a good price for the information,' said Veto hopefully.

'You won't get it from me,' said Meenu firmly.

Just then the Masked Avenger came out of the caravan.

'Right!' she announced. 'I'm here! Let's go!'

'First, I'd better tell you what we're looking for –' began Lord Veto.

'Princess Ava's already told me,' said the Masked Avenger. 'It's the Royal Troll Ring, right?'

'Yes,' said Meenu.

'Then let's get started! Lead on, Veto!'

'That's *Lord* Veto to you,' said Veto sniffily.

'Whatever,' shrugged the Avenger. 'Just move it, buster!'

'What an uncouth person,' muttered Lord Veto to Meenu. 'I find it hard to think that Princess Ava is a friend to this dreadful creature.'

'The ring!' hissed Meenu urgently.

'Of course,' said Veto. 'This way!'

And he hurried towards the back entrance to the castle, Meenu and the Avenger following.


Warg moved swiftly along the tunnel that ran deep beneath Veto Castle to the prison cells, with Hunk close behind, and Milo hurrying to keep up.

'I wonder how many trolls they'll have on guard,' muttered Milo.

Warg pulled to a halt at a corner, and the
hurrying Hunk and Milo crashed forward into
him. Warg peered round the corner.

'Three,' he whispered.

'Three what?' asked Hunk.

'Trolls on guard,' said Warg. And he gestured
with his claw.

Hunk and Milo peered carefully round the
corner and saw three huge Trolls standing guard
outside a cell door.

'Great!' smiled Hunk. 'One troll each!'

'Er . . .' began Milo doubtfully.

'Don't worry,' Hunk reassured him. 'Warg and I can take them all, can't we, Warg?'

'Tag-team!' said Warg.

'Exactly!' nodded Hunk.

'So what do we *do*, exactly?' asked Milo.

'Well, firstly, we do our best to avoid unnecessary violence,' said Hunk.

Warg looked at Hunk, puzzled.

'But you're a wrestler,' he said.

'Yes, but wrestling is a sport,' said Hunk. 'It combines the art of movement with science and skill. Violence shouldn't be a part of it.'

'Well, if we're not going to use violence, what are we going to do?' asked Milo.

'Reason with them,' said Hunk. 'Leave it to me.'

He left the safety of the corner and strode along the corridor to the cell door where the three huge trolls stood guard.

'Good day!' he greeted them cheerfully. 'My name is Hunk and I am a Wrestling Troll. You have my friend and wrestling partner, Big Rock, in that cell. I'd be most obliged if you'd let him out. And also our orc friend, Dunk, who's in there with him.'

The three trolls studied Hunk, bewilderment on their faces.

'You troll?' asked one.

'Half-troll,' said Hunk. 'And proud of it. So, how about it? If you'll just open the door –'

'Go away!' snarled one of the trolls.

Hunk shook his head sadly.

'My purpose,' he said, 'is to avoid unnecessary violence –'

Hunk never finished his sentence. The troll nearest to him suddenly let fly with a swinging punch aimed straight at Hunk's head.

*CRUNCH!!*

That was the sound of the troll guard's fist bashing another of the guards, because with amazing speed Hunk had grabbed the nearest troll and brought him in front of him to act as a shield. Hunk let go of the troll, who collapsed unconscious to the ground. The remaining two trolls stared down at their fallen comrade, stunned.

'Warg!' called Hunk. 'It's two against two now!'

Warg hurtled down the corridor and there was a blur of clothes and beak and claws. Warg grabbed the nearest troll, turned him upside down and crunched him head first into the ground. Meanwhile, Hunk had taken hold of the remaining troll, swung him over his shoulder in a throw, and then fallen on him, pinning him to the ground.

'There's some rope hanging on a hook here, Milo!' called Hunk. 'Tie them up!'

Milo came hurrying to join them. He took the coil of rope from the hook and set to work with Hunk and Warg, tying the three trolls together.

'There!' said Warg.

'I thought you said you didn't want to use unnecessary violence,' commented Milo.

'And I didn't,' said Hunk. 'That was necessary violence. A different thing all together.'

He took the keys from the fallen trolls and unlocked the cell door. Out of the cell came a small, thin, frail-looking old orc.

'Hello,' he wheezed. 'My name's Speedfoot. Thank you for rescuing me.'

'Our pleasure,' said Milo. He called into the cell: 'Come on, Big Rock and Dunk! We haven't got time to hang about!'

Speedfoot looked at him, puzzled.

'Who are you talking to?' he asked. 'I was the only one in there. They locked me up because I protested about them turning us orcs off the place.'

Milo, Hunk and Warg looked at one another, bewildered. Then Milo dropped to his knees beside the one conscious troll.

'Where are Big Rock and Dunk the orc?' he demanded.

'Oh, those two,' said the troll. 'Massive had them taken along to the wrestling match. He said he's going to kill them in front of everyone, right after he kills that little kid, Jack.'

'What?' burst out Hunk, horrified. 'We have

to get to the wrestling match!'

'And that's exactly where you're going!' said a voice behind them.

They looked round and saw that several ninjas had appeared and were pointing swords at them.

'We can take them, Warg!' yelled Hunk.

The nearest ninja moved his sword with incredible swiftness so that the blade pointed at Milo.

'Try it, and he dies first!' he said.

Jack and Robin crept along the corridor towards the Big Hall where Massive had held court and given his deadly judgement on Big Rock and Dunk. Or rather, Jack crept; Robin did his best to creep but his hooves still click-clacked on the hard floor.

'They'll know we're coming!' whispered Jack, stopping at a bend in the corridor. 'They'll hear you!'

'It's not my fault,' whispered back Robin. 'I'm a horse. Horses have hooves!' Then he smiled. 'Actually, that gives me an idea! Stay here!'

'Why?' asked Jack. 'You won't be able to defeat the guards on your own.'

'Trust me,' said Robin confidently.

Robin headed off along the corridor, while Jack remained in hiding behind the corner. Jack peered out to see what Robin was up to, ready to rush to his friend's aid.

There was just one troll guard on duty outside the Big Hall. The troll turned towards Robin as the old horse came near.

'Halt!' ordered the troll.

Robin pulled to a halt.

'Okay,' said Robin. 'I've halted. Now what?'

'You shouldn't be here,' said the troll.

'Why?' asked Robin.

'Because this is private,' said the troll.

'Oh. Okay,' nodded Robin. 'I'll go. But before I do, would you have a look at my rear hoof?'

'Why?' asked the troll.

'Because I think I've got something stuck on it,' said Robin.

He turned round so that his rear end was to the troll and lifted one of his back legs. The troll bent down and peered at the hoof.

'No,' said the troll. 'Nothing on it.'

'No,' said Robin. 'But here's something much more dangerous.'

And with that, he let out a fart. The troll gave a cough and then crashed to the ground, out cold.

'I'm sorry about that,' Robin apologised to the unconscious troll. 'It was in very bad taste, but this is an emergency.'

Jack came hurrying along the corridor to join him.

'Wow!' said Jack. 'That was incredible.'

'Horse farts,' sighed Robin. 'The most potent weapon we have. Luckily we don't use it very often.'

Jack pushed open the door and he and Robin hurried into the room. Blaze was still there, huddled beneath the metal net, looking very miserable. Jack snatched the net and threw it to one side. Immediately, Blaze flared into a

flash of light, and before Jack's and Robin's eyes he changed swiftly into a variety of shapes: dragon, bird, snake, horse, and then back to his own phoenix shape again.

'Thank you!' burst out Blaze. 'I thought that net was going to be the end of me!'

'Now you're free, I suggest you go and help Ava and the others search for the ring,' said Jack. 'They're going to need your help. You can change into all sorts of shapes and go into places they can't.'

'Right,' said Blaze. And he turned into a mouse. 'What about you?' he asked.

Jack sighed.

'I've got a wrestling match against a massive troll to get to,' he said unhappily.

# CHAPTER 7

Lord Veto, Meenu and the Masked Avenger pulled up outside a large dark wooden door on which an ornamental crown made of fake gold had been fixed, complete with imitation jewels that sparkled.

'Oh, how tacky!' said Lord Veto in disgust. 'I am shocked!'

'How did you know this would be Massive's room?' asked Meenu suspiciously.

'Because it used to be my private room,' sniffed Lord Veto. 'It's the finest and most beautiful room in the whole castle. It was obvious that Massive would choose it.' He pointed at the crown fixed to the door with deep distaste. 'But if this is the sort of thing he does, I dread to think what it looks like inside now.'

'One way to find out,' said the Masked Avenger. She tried the door handle and scowled. 'It's locked. I'm going to have to kick it down.'

'Don't you dare!' said Veto. 'That door is ancient and very valuable!'

'But it's not yours any more,' Meenu pointed out.

'It will be one day, once I have my own back

on those treacherous Voyadis,' said Veto grimly. 'When Jack takes his rightful place as Troll King, we'll raise a powerful army of Wrestling Trolls that will crush the Voyadis and restore this place to me!'

'Yes, but in the meantime, how do we get in?' demanded the Masked Avenger.

There was a jangling sound, and they saw that Lord Veto had produced a bunch of keys from his pocket.

'They may have kicked me out of this place, but they didn't know I kept a spare set of keys,' he said smugly.

He selected a key and unlocked the door.

'Careful,' warned the Avenger. 'We don't know what's inside.'

'I expect there'll be some very tacky furniture and some dreadful curtains,' sniffed Veto, pushing open the door.

The three entered the room. As they did, they heard a low growl.

'And a Horror Hound,' whispered Meenu nervously.

A large animal – part huge dog, part wolf – had risen from where it had been lying near the fireplace, and its yellow eyes were now glaring directly at them, its large, sharp teeth bared in a snarl.

'I think we have to leave!' gulped Lord Veto, and he went to dart back out of the room, but was stopped by the Masked Avenger, who grabbed him and hauled him back.

'Oh no you don't!' she said. 'We're here to get the ring and save Jack!'

With that, she kicked the door shut.

'Are you sure that was a good idea?' asked Meenu. 'Now we're trapped in here with it!'

The Horror Hound moved slowly towards them, growling.

'Sit!' ordered Lord Veto desperately. 'Down!'

The Hound kept coming.

'I don't think it's taking any notice of you,' muttered Meenu unhappily.

Suddenly the huge creature let out a growl and leapt at them, its mouth open wide, saliva dripping from its vicious-looking teeth.

'Look out!' shouted the Avenger, and she pushed Lord Veto and Meenu so that they toppled to the floor. At the same time she threw herself towards the attacking Hound, grabbing the creature around the neck with both hands as its jaws closed on the top of her head.

*SMACK!*

The Masked Avenger slammed the creature head first into the hard floor, knocking it out.

'There!' said the Avenger triumphantly.

'Er . . .' said Meenu, and she pointed awkwardly at the unconscious Hound's mouth.

The Avenger looked and saw that her mask was gripped between the creature's teeth.

'Princess Ava!' The words burst out from Lord Veto in shock as he pushed himself to his feet and stared, pointing at her, bewildered and stunned. '*You* are the Masked Avenger!'

'Well . . . yes,' admitted Ava, realising she could hardly deny it.

'You! A royal person! A princess!' continued the shocked Veto indignantly.

'Yes, all right,' said Ava sourly. 'Now you know. Get over it.' She picked up her mask and strapped it back on her head, then glared at him warningly. 'But it's still a secret! If you dare tell anyone –'

'No, no!' said Lord Veto. 'Far be it from me to give away your secret!' Then he smiled to himself. After this was over, he'd find a way to put this new information to a profitable purpose . . . He shook his head, still stunned at the discovery. 'A princess. Wrestling. Whatever next!'

'Jack's a prince and he wrestles,' pointed out Meenu.

'And my father was a wrestler before he became King of Weevil,' added Ava. She grinned. 'I reckon we've got enough royal wrestlers to make up a royal tag team!'

'Unthinkable!' shuddered Lord Veto.

'Can we talk about this later?' said Meenu. She pointed at the unconscious Horror Hound. 'For one thing, I think we ought to tie this creature up in case it wakes while we're still searching. And for another, if we don't find this ring quickly, Jack will be in deep trouble. He'll be entering the ring against Massive at any moment!'

# CHAPTER 8

The large purpose-built arena in the grounds
of the castle where Veto had put on his
wrestling tournaments was packed. But
whereas, in Lord Veto's time, most of the
wrestlers and the crowd had been made up of
orcs, now the Wrestling Hall was packed with
trolls. The only orcs in the place, Jack noticed
as he and Robin peered into the arena, were
Dunk and Warg. Dunk was at the back of the
arena, bound to Big Rock with heavy metal
chains that wound around them both. They
were being guarded by six trolls armed with
clubs. Next to them, also chained together,
were Milo, Hunk and Warg, guarded by the
armed ninjas.

'Looks like there's no chance of you getting any help from them,' murmured Robin.

'I know,' muttered Jack. 'Let's hope that Ava and the others can find the ring.'

A small troll had climbed into the ring. He strode to the centre and held up his hands to silence the excited chatter.

'Fellow trolls!' he announced. 'Troll ladies and gentlemen! Welcome to one of the most exciting and important wrestling matches that has ever been held anywhere! This is truly a match of life and death! In the red corner I give you your very own King of the Trolls – Massive!'

A huge roar of appreciation went up from the crowd as the huge troll stepped into the arena, which soon gave way to the sound of troll feet stamping, and loud cheering and whistling. Massive leapt into the ring, then paraded around it, waving at the crowd. On his head he wore a gold crown, and a purple cloak hung from his shoulders.

'He's not shy, is he?' muttered Robin.

The referee waved his hands to quieten the crowd, and then announced: 'And his opponent, in the blue corner, the pretender to the throne, who claims he is a half-troll: Jack the kitchen boy!'

'That's all wrong!' burst out Jack angrily. 'I'm not after the throne! And I'm not a kitchen boy any more!'

'Getting angry is good,' nodded Robin. 'It might make you turn into Thud. Any signs of it?' he asked hopefully.

'No,' admitted Jack.

The crowd was getting restless and had started chanting, 'Jack! Jack! We're waiting!'

'I'd better get on with it,' sighed Jack. 'Wish me luck.'

With that, Jack strode down the aisle to the ring, where Massive and the referee were waiting. As he did so the chanting changed and became boos, getting louder and louder, so that by the time Jack pulled himself into the ring the whole arena was a thunderstorm of booing and angry shouts.

It looked an unlikely pairing: Massive was about twice the height of Jack, and more than twice as wide, with huge muscles of granite that shone in his rocky body. As Massive took off his cloak and crown, he revealed his costume: expensive threads of gold decorating a red costume, with a large golden crown on the chest, covered with jewels.

Next to him, Jack made a pitiful figure: small, thin, pale and frail-looking, wearing a worn and patched costume of faded grey.

'Troll ladies and gentlemen!' announced the referee. 'I did not exaggerate when I said this bout is a matter of life and death! The rules are the same as always: two pinfalls or submissions, or a knockout, to decide the winner. If Massive wins then the traitor Big Rock, the treacherous orc Dunk, and the pretender, Jack, will die here! But if Jack wins, then Big Rock and Dunk will be spared and Massive will stand down as king and leave the way clear for Jack to become King of the Trolls!'

'No!' howled the troll audience. 'Down with Jack! Massive for ever!'

Through the shouting, Jack heard Big Rock call out: 'Jack true Troll King!'

Jack looked towards where Big Rock and Dunk were being kept prisoner, and saw the troll guards leap on them and tie a gag over Big Rock's mouth.

The referee ordered Massive and Jack to their corners, and then pointed to the troll at the ringside operating the bell.

*DING!*

The match had begun.

# CHAPTER 9

'It's no good!' groaned Meenu. 'The ring isn't here!'

'And I've checked every small nook and tiny cranny in this room,' said Blaze as he changed back from a tiny mouse into his usual phoenix shape. He had come scurrying under the door a few minutes earlier to help them search. 'It's in none of them.'

'But it must be!' raged Veto. 'It's the most precious thing that Massive has got! Where else would he keep it except in his private bedroom!'

The Masked Avenger stopped rummaging through yet another wardrobe and turned to them, her mouth open, stunned as the realisation hit her.

'That's it!' she burst out.

'What's it?' asked Meenu.

'The ring is too precious for Massive to leave *anywhere*!'

Meenu stared at her as she realised what the Masked Avenger had worked out.

'You mean that Massive has got the ring on him?' she asked.

'Yes!' nodded the Avenger.

'Of course!' exclaimed Lord Veto. 'That's brilliant! So cunning and clever!'

'So . . . how are we going to let Jack know?' asked Meenu. 'As soon as we appear in the arena, the trolls will grab us.'

'I'll do it,' said Blaze. And he turned into a tiny blue fly and flew out of the room.

The crowd booed loudly as once again Jack darted between Massive's legs and rolled clear of the huge troll. It was a tactic Jack had used to keep himself out of trouble during the opening minutes of the bout. He had danced nimbly about the ring, keeping away from the huge Troll's clutching hands, and when Massive had managed to imprison Jack in a corner, Jack had dropped down and rolled swiftly between the troll's legs, and then jumped up the other side. Jack knew that if it came to a contest of strength, he would lose. His only hope was to stay out of trouble until Ava arrived with the ring and he could slip it on his finger and turn into Thud.

'Stay still, you little squirt!' hissed Massive.

The huge troll reached out and Jack skipped to one side, but as he did so he bumped into the referee and stumbled unsteadily back towards Massive.

*WHUMP!*

Massive took the opportunity, grabbed Jack by the neck, lifted him up and slammed him down hard onto the canvas, knocking all the air out of him. As Jack struggled to recover, Massive flipped Jack onto his back and fell on him, pinning him firmly to the canvas.

'One!' shouted the crowd joyfully.

'Two!' continued the referee. 'Three!'

The audience erupted into wild cheering as Massive leapt to his feet and jumped heavily around the ring.

'First pinfall to Massive!' shouted the referee. 'One more pinfall or submission and Massive wins!'

Painfully, Jack pushed himself up. His whole body ached from where the huge troll had fallen on him, but he saw Massive reaching for him again to finish the bout and managed to dance back out of his reach.

Suddenly he heard a low buzzing sound, and saw that a fly had appeared and settled on Massive's nose.

Annoyed, the troll flicked at the fly with his huge hand. The fly moved away and flew towards Jack. Suddenly there was a flash of light, and the fly had transformed into a phoenix.

'Blaze!' gasped Jack.

'Massive's got the ring on him!' exclaimed Blaze.

There was a roar of anger from Massive, and

the next second the troll swung his huge arm, his granite fist smashing into Blaze and crashing the phoenix unconscious to the canvas.

Jack stared at Massive, and at the decorative gold crown on the front of the Troll's costume, and suddenly saw that the ring – *his* ring – had been sewn to it among the jewels. Jack reached out for the ring, but as his fingers touched it, Massive swung his arm again, catching Jack on the side of the head and sending him crashing back against the ropes.

Jack hung on the ropes, his head pounding painfully from the punch. As he hung there he saw Massive stomp over to where Blaze was laying on the canvas. The huge troll lifted one of his enormous feet and then crashed it down on the phoenix, crushing it.

'No!'

Tears leapt into Jack's eyes as Massive stepped back and Jack saw the mangled body of the phoenix lying there. Jack's tears were blinding him, he could barely see through them, but he was aware that Massive was coming back at him – he could just make out the huge troll's shape as he got nearer. Only Massive didn't seem so huge any more. In fact, the troll seemed to be shrinking, because now Jack was looking *down* on Massive. And his tears weren't wet any more; they were more like a film of transparent quartz over his eyes.

*RAAAAAARRRRR!!!!!!*

In the ring, Massive looked up in shock at the huge troll that had taken the place of Jack. The audience gasped. The referee backed away.

*GRRRAAAAARRRRRR!!!!*

Thud, the giant troll grabbed the stunned Massive with both of his huge hands and dashed him to the canvas, then dropped on him, pinning him to the floor.

'Count!' came the shout from Dunk. 'The rules say you must count!'

'One!' began the referee. 'Two! Three!'

Thud rolled off Massive and pushed himself to his feet. He reached down and picked up the stunned troll, lifting him clear of the canvas, then stood him up.

Massive stared at Thud, petrified by shock, his mouth and eyes wide open. Then he began to back away from the enormous troll, but before he could take more than two steps, Thud had grabbed hold of him and thrown him up in the air. As Massive came down, Thud caught him, slammed him into the canvas, then fell on him, pinning him down.

The audience were stunned into silence. The referee gulped, then counted: 'One! Two! Three! I declare the winner is . . . er . . . Jack!'

'Thud!' shouted Big Rock from the back, spitting the gag out of his mouth.

'Jack – Thud!' stammered the referee.

To gasps of awe from the audience, the enormous figure of Thud shimmered, and then shrank, and then the frail-looking figure of Jack stood in the ring once more.

'Just Jack,' he said. He reached down and took his ring from the crown sewn on Massive's chest. 'And I'll have my ring back, thank you very much.'

Then, from the hushed, stunned audience, a voice called out: 'Jack is the true King of the Trolls!' Then another voice could be heard echoing the cry. Someone else shouted, 'Jack is King!' and the cry was taken up, echoing around the arena: 'Jack is King! Jack is King!'

Big Rock looked at the others and smiled.

'Yes!' he said proudly. 'Jack King!'

# CHAPTER 10

Jack and the gang watched as Massive and his entourage of trolls marched out through one side of the gateway of Veto Castle, while families of orcs wheeled their belongings back in on their carts. Blaze, now recovered, flew overhead, making patterns in the sky.

'I'm a phoenix,' he'd said to Jack after the match. 'I die and then I'm reborn! You don't need to worry about me as much as you do!'

Jack was pleased to see that plenty of trolls had decided to stay behind in the grounds, and were even now welcoming the orcs back and helping them carry their belongings back into their houses. The first thing many of the orcs did was put the kettle on, and outside many of the houses orcs and trolls sat around on chairs and wooden boxes, chatting and drinking tea. Hunk was very busy, going from house to house, talking to everyone, putting them at their ease and carrying heavy furniture in and out when it was needed.

'Orcs and trolls together,' nodded Big Rock. 'Now Massive gone, trolls not scared to be friends with orcs any more.' He smiled at Jack. 'Jack good king. Trolls follow his example.'

'I'm not the King,' protested Jack.

'Yes you are,' said Princess Ava. 'You're the heir to the throne, and I'm afraid you can't get out of it.'

'And the trolls need someone like you to be king,' added Meenu. 'There wouldn't have been anything like this, trolls and orcs sitting happily together, if Massive had still been king.'

'You should have had him executed,' growled Lord Veto. 'That's what he planned for you!'

'You don't bring people together by fighting,' said Jack. 'If people are going to learn to live together, it starts with forgiving your enemy.'

As he said these words, he took a deep breath, then added with feeling, 'Like I forgive you, grandfather.'

'Jack!' exclaimed Lord Veto, touched. 'I don't deserve it!'

'No, you don't,' Robin snorted.

Jack smiled, and then added, 'And Massive could have stayed here if he'd wanted to. I told him he could.'

Milo shook his head. 'That was never going to happen. Massive is scared of Thud and knows he can never beat him. He's also scared of the Voyadis – and with good reason. He let them down. He didn't only lose the crown and Veto Castle, he lost the Troll Homeland.'

'I saw the ninjas sneak off after Massive left,' said Ava. 'My guess is they're going to take revenge on Massive on behalf of the Voyadis.'

'And once they've dealt with Massive, they'll come after Jack . . .' said Meenu, worried.

'We'll face that when it comes,' said Jack.

'So, what are your plans now you're officially King of the Trolls?' asked Milo.

'Well, I thought I'd abdicate,' said Jack. 'You know, step down from being king.'

'You can't!' said Ava. 'If you do, Massive could come back and claim the throne again, and there'll be all that trouble once more.'

'The princess is right,' said Robin.

'Okay,' said Jack. 'In that case, I'll be Prince Jack. I can still go off on my travels with Waldo's Wrestling Trolls.'

'But what about the throne?' asked Meenu.

'I'll appoint a regent to look after the throne for me until I'm ready to come back and take it over.'

'What regent?' asked Big Rock, puzzled.

'Someone who's appointed to look after the throne until the heir to the throne is ready to be king,' boomed Lord Veto. 'May I say that is an excellent idea!'

'You approve?' asked Jack.

'Absolutely!' said Veto. 'Traditionally, of course, it is a member of the ruler-to-be's family who takes on the role of regent for them. An uncle. Or, say, perhaps a grandfather.'

And he smiled broadly.

'True,' nodded Jack, 'but what I was thinking of . . .'

Just then Hunk reappeared with a huge grin.

'It looks like everyone's settled in,' he announced. 'And all the trolls I've spoken to are very happy with the way things have turned out.'

'That's because you make the trolls and orcs feel happy about living here together, Hunk,' smiled Jack. 'That's why I'd like you to be my regent.'

'What!' exploded Lord Veto.

Hunk frowned. 'What's a regent?' he asked.

'It's . . . ME!' raged Lord Veto.

'No it isn't,' said Jack.

Briefly, he explained to Hunk what a regent was. At the end of it, Hunk looked doubtful.

'It doesn't seem right,' he said.

'It isn't right!' exploded Lord Veto. 'He's not of royal blood!'

'That doesn't matter,' said Jack. 'Lots of people who aren't of royal blood become

knights and things. And Hunk is half-troll.'
He turned back to Hunk. 'Please say you'll
do it. That way I know the kingdom will be
a happy and safe place while I'm away
from it.'

Hunk looked around at the others. All of

them, with the exception of Lord Veto, were nodding, urging him to say yes.

'In that case: yes,' said Hunk. 'I shall be honoured.'

'And what about me?' exploded Lord Veto. 'Where do I go? What do I do?'

'You could always come along with us,' suggested Milo. 'Be part of Waldo's Wrestling Trolls.'

'We make room in caravan for you,' nodded Big Rock.

'Me in a *caravan*?' echoed Lord Veto, shocked.

'Actually, there's no need for that,' said Jack. 'In fact, there's no need for you to go anywhere. It would help Hunk if he had someone here who knew the place, who could help look after it.'

'A caretaker,' nodded Milo. 'Good idea.'

'A *caretaker*!' repeated Lord Veto with distaste.

'You could stay in the castle,' said Hunk. 'It's too big for me. I'd be happy in a small cottage.'

Lord Veto's expression turned thoughtful.

'Will Warg be able to stay with me?' he asked.

'Of course,' said Hunk. 'And every time Waldo's Wrestling Trolls, or Princess Ava, or anyone else, comes to visit, they can stay there as well.'

'I think I'd rather be in our caravan,' said Jack.

'Well, that's decided then!' smiled Milo. 'Waldo's Wrestling Trolls are still on the road!'

Princess Ava grinned and nudged Jack in the ribs.

'Perhaps we can make up a royal tag team,' she whispered. 'The Masked Avenger and Thud; the Prince and Princess of Wrestling.'

'Outrageous!' snorted Lord Veto.

'Well, if we're going on the road, we'd better get a move on,' said Milo. 'Come on, Big Rock and Robin. Let's get the caravan hitched up.'

'We'd better get on the road ourselves,' Ava said to Meenu. 'The people of Weevil will be wondering what's happened to us.'

As they departed to get their caravans ready for their journeys, Jack turned to Dunk.

'Thanks, Dunk,' he said. 'If you hadn't come and warned us what was happening, this could have turned out badly.'

'You'll be a good Troll King, Jack,' said Dunk.

'And you and your family can have a home here as long as you want, Dunk,' said Hunk. Then a thought struck him. 'Dunk and Hunk. It sounds like a good name for a tag team.'

The sound of rolling wheels arriving interrupted them.

'We're all ready, Jack,' said Milo. Then he grinned. '*Prince* Jack.'

Jack laughed.

'Just Jack,' he said.

He patted Robin, and then climbed up onto the driving seat and made himself comfortable next to Milo.

'Let's go!' he said.

With a creak of old wood, Robin pulled the wagon and it began to head towards the gateway. Big Rock ran alongside it and Blaze flew overhead. As they made their way through the castle gateway and onto the open road, the sound of singing floated back from the caravan:

'Wrestling Trolls
Tum-di-dum!
Wrestling Trolls
Tum-di-dum!'

Thank you for choosing a Hot Key book.

If you want to know more about our authors
and what we publish, you can find us online.

You can start at our website

**www.hotkeybooks.com**

And you can also find us on:

**We hope to see you soon!**

**Lovereading4kids reader reviews of**
**Wrestling Trolls Match 1: Big Rock and the Masked Avenger**
**by Jim Eldridge**

'I really like *Wrestling Trolls*. I really like Robin the horse because he talks, Big Rock because he's nice, Jack because he saves Princess Ava, and Princess Ava because she wrestles!'

Richie, age 7

'*Wrestling Trolls* is an action-packed book with awesome wrestling moves. The characters are clever and funny. I loved the story and can't wait to read the next instalment.'

Jacob, age 9

'The story had funny parts, action and good characters. Some of my favourite parts were Jack turning into a wrestling troll and I liked Robin the horse because he was grumpy and helpful.'

Jack, age 8

'It was brilliant! I liked how Jack changed into Thud - I won't tell you what Thud is so I don't give away the story . . . I really liked the song and keep singing it.'

George, age 7

'*Wrestling Trolls* is exciting because it is full of action. This book is fantastic if you like lots of wrestling and people being rescued from bad guys.'

Thomas, age 7

'I give it 10/10 even though I don't like wrestling, because I liked the story!'

Alexander, age 8